Rony Jane was born in Sofia, Bulgaria in 1983. She was a lonely and an unhappy kid. That's why she started writing her diary. This helped her to develop her imagination. In 2015, she applied to Sunderland University to study creative writing. Unfortunately, she did not finish because she did not have enough money. After that, she moved to Birmingham, found her love and gave birth to her daughter. In 2019, she started writing her first book because she wanted her daughter to be proud of her one day. Her first book was published in April 2021.

Rony Jane

EDMUND STREET

AUSTIN MACAULEY PUBLISHERS™

LONDON · CAMBRIDGE · NEW YORK · SHARJAH

A CIP catalogue record for this title is available from the British Library.

ISBN 9781398422957 (Paperback)
ISBN 9781398436572 (ePub e-book)

www.austinmacauley.com

First Published 2022
Austin Macauley Publishers Ltd®
1 Canada Square
Canary Wharf
London
E14 5AA

To my teacher in life and art, Svetoslav Dobrev, who helped me to develop my skills and who was absolutely dedicated when I was in my teenage years. Thank you, teacher.

July 16th was a very hot day. The height of summer was felt more than anywhere else in the city centre, which was empty these days. A lot of people had gone on holiday. The sun had risen high, and it was bearing down heavily. The few people who moved on the streets seemed tired. Friday was a tiring day but also helped everyone to unwind – it was the last of the week, but the beginning of the weekend.

Right at 12:50 pm, Valerie came out of her little flat. Not typically for a 21-year-old girl, she was wearing a blue suit and a white shirt and had dark gloves on, in spite of the warm weather. Valerie locked the massive door and walked up the street. Her long, blond, straight hair was tied in a ponytail, her eyes were emerald blue, and she had a small, snub nose and beautiful thick lips. On her gorgeous face was a stern determination.

She was a tall and slender girl, more than 173 cm in height. She definitely caught the eye, and now seemed even more impressive—with her clothing and gloves in this hot weather. It was exactly 1:12 pm when she arrived at the door of 148 Edmund Street Despite the heat and long walk, Valerie still looked fresh. She looked at her watch and waited for exactly two minutes before she knocked on the door. At 1:15 pm, two taps were clearly heard and exactly 40 seconds were needed for the hostess to open the door.

148 Edmund Street was a massive building from the beginning of the 20th century. The yard was wide and a narrow path led to massive columns, which then led to the front door. There were many trees and shrubs, but as a good hostess, the missis had hired a gardener and everything was trimmed with meticulous precision. Every bush and blade looked impeccable. The front door was made of solid wood, and the house itself had nine apartments divided into two floors.

On the top floor there were attics, but for years, no one had been up there to see what was going on. The house was made of brick and there were countless windows. Large and long corridors connected the two wings of the building. The walls inside and outside were white, and the carpet was thick and dense in material, and grey in colour. The whole building was well-maintained and cleaned daily.

Mrs Mackgraver opened the door. She was 72 years old and not more than 153 cm tall. She was a weak woman, with short-cropped and completely white hair. She was the only owner of the house called Grove Village. She had a little face, with wrinkled skin, blue eyes and thin lips. Her forehead was narrow and unsurely. She had a pretty provocative look despite her little physique. Even as a younger woman, she had never looked attractive, but her posture was of a woman with great self-esteem.

This was her explanation: she was born in a wealthy family and this self-esteem came from all previous generations. Her father was a prominent lawyer in Newcastle at the beginning of the century. He had graduated in London, but had returned to his hometown to practice. Mr Mackgraver had a very busy practice and after working with wealthy clients for more than 30 years, he was able to gain a fortune with his earned deeds. Her mother, Mrs Mackgraver, though not so much a noble housewife, was proud of the accomplishments of the household. Mrs Mackgraver was an only child of these parents, for the simple reason that only she survived from among seven children (the others were born healthy but died before they reached two years of age). She was raised as a spoilt brat, given her best education and learned everything she could buy with money – riding, literature, and languages. She was proud of her descent and was also the proud owner of Grove Village on 148 Edmund Street.

Already 72 years old, this woman felt the weight of her age and for this reason, and maybe some others, had hired Valerie to clean her house. Because of her very difficult personality she never got married and had no children. Besides Valerie Smith, she paid the gardener every week to keep the garden and bushes in good shape. Mrs Mackgraver was just a meticulous woman with a lot of money to spend. When she went to open the door, the old lady did not express any emotion, just pulled back slightly so that the girl could enter.

"Good afternoon, Mrs Mackgraver," said Valerie.

"Good afternoon, Miss Smith," answered Mrs Mackgraver.

The old lady preferred to speak to everyone by using their last name, so that she wouldn't get too close to people from the staff.

"You know your duties for today. Right at 4:15 pm, I will expect you here to hand me the keys and pay you for the week."

Despite the unnecessary reservation, Valerie was pleased with the pay, and the work was not at all difficult. Valerie Smith was a first-year forensic student at the University of Durham. She had just graduated the year, and had one duty. It was to come to Grove Village on Tuesday and Friday and spend three hours of her time cleaning up the house. As a student from Eastern Europe without a history in England, she had searched for a job for almost six months. The only places she was offered jobs were as a waitress in a pub at the minimum wage and this one.

When she heard the pay and the hours she did not hesitate to accept. Despite the popular stereotype that being from Easter Europe could only help you end up like a cleaner in this country, she did not mind the easy money.

She was only 21 and hoped she had a future. She believed it was the transition that would help her get stable financially and become the greatest investigator around.

The strange thing was that she was supposed to be cleaning up the part of the house that was never used. Despite the many rooms in the Grove Village, there were only six people. Mrs Mackgraver had a separate flat on the ground floor where nobody was allowed to enter. The other five people lived in one wing on the second floor. The left wing was empty for years, but the old owner gave the keys to Valerie twice a week and expected flawless purity to be maintained. So Valerie opened the rooms one by one and in the three hours maintained their impeccable appearance.

For a girl like her, who had descended from a normal family with few high incomes and came abroad to develop herself, it was a dream. She received enough money to be able to pay the rent, eat and send a little bit to her mother.

There really was no prestige in this. Being a cleaning lady did not bring you many dividends, but for now Valerie was not so fussy about this. The job actually had found her alone at the beginning of the school year in November and for eight months she had been coming to this house.

She had not imagined, while coming to England, that she and many of her fellow citizens would perform such work, but hoped that the time spent here would not be lost.

One of the things that puzzled her was the requirement of clothing and, in particular, to wear a certain kind of suit and gloves, trousers and white shirt. The old lady did not care what the weather was out there, warm or cold. She always required this outfit.

The suits that were bought from the old lady. Despite these quirks, the pay prevailed, and so Valerie with persistence had been dealing with this house for almost a year now.

The rooms in Grove Village were very similar. In each of them the carpet was thick and grey, the beds had red covers, and the bedside tables had a golden lamp. The bathrooms were large—with marble slabs and huge bathtubs. The house was built to be filled with delight. At one end there was a living room with a huge library. There was something romantic about the fireplace next to so many books.

Most of the time the job didn't need very much work. Valerie cleaned for about two hours, going around all the rooms and then going to the living room. Then she would sit in a large instructed chair and spend exactly an hour there. She'd take a book or look at the books themselves on the shelves. There was mostly law literature, but since it was during work hours she was definitely interested in the different cases. Sometimes she felt a little guilty that she was paid for that hour, but she was passing it like this. After all, Mrs Mackgraver gave her such a meaningless job. At 4:15 pm, Valerie knocked on the door of the housekeeper's apartment. Even though she had been working there for so long, Valerie had never been inside.

Usually Mrs McGraw would go out and settle her bills in the living room on the ground floor. Valerie was required to sign into the book for £400 a week.

"Tell me why she pays you so much for this job?" her classmate Johnny asked her that same day.

"Honestly, I have no idea," Valerie replied.

That night, the two were sitting in a pub, with Valerie having promised to pay the bill. John had been her friend since the beginning of the school year. They both went to the same class and were excellent. Forensics was the right thing for them because they shared this passion. They went out for a drink quite often.

John Burton was a tall, slender young man. Brown, warm eyes, high forehead, small nose and protruding chin finished his image. John didn't like Valerie *that* way; it was more of a deep affection and friendship for a soul mate.

"Tell me about her again, there must be something that made an impression on you that's not right. Can there be anything that makes her pay you such a high wage?"

"I told you what she looked like, you know about her strange habits of wearing a suit and gloves. Nothing new has happened lately," Valerie said. "We hardly talk, sometimes I wonder how she's been through those 72 years and hasn't communicated with anyone."

"There must be something," insisted Johnny. "Val, you're going to have to look around, and her tenants, what kind of people are they? Tell me about them."

"Let's order dinner first," Valerie said, "and then I'll tell you."

Valerie ordered both pizza and chips with a beer. It had been 10 minutes since dinner started when Valerie started talking.

"As far as I'm familiar, Johnny, only five people live in the house, and that's how it has been for years. Mrs Mackgraver doesn't like to change tenants. When I started there at the end of November last year I saw those people, but since then I have hardly talked with them. They live in the other wing anyway. But that doesn't stop me from shaking up for information."

"Are you doing that?" Johnny asked that. "That's going to be great. You know, Val, we can practice all summer and prepare for the new school year. I think psychology will be of any use to you in this case."

"Well, John, even though I'm not so sure something's going on there, let's do this, me and you are on this case. I'll carry the information, and then we'll both analyse it. We'll meet every Friday and Saturday so we can discuss it. But if within a month we fail to gather such information that is interesting and important, we give up."

"Val, I'm telling you, there's something. Look, I got a job at a catering agency, and I have to go along with the management to work on Thursdays, Fridays and Saturdays. Let our meetings be on Sunday and Monday. Then we're both free."

"I agree, let's finish eating, pay and go to a bar for a drink."

"Which I'm going to pay for," Johnny interrupted her.

"That's good," Valerie said, "this bill is for me, the next one is for you."

When they reached the entrance to the bar, there was already a queue outside. They lined up and waited for their turn to come.

Valerie came to her apartment shortly after midnight. Despite drinking cocktails; she felt her brain to be completely sober. Before she fell asleep, she wanted to set up her jobs for next Tuesday.

She certainly wouldn't have been able to find out all five roommates at once, but for a few days she'd known who lived where in the house. She went to bed and fell asleep blissfully, looking forward to the rest of the summer.

On Tuesday, Valerie repeated the same procedure. At 12:50 pm, she left the flat and at 1:12 pm, she was at the door of the house. At 1:15 pm, she knocked on the door. Mrs Mackgraver didn't take long today. When she saw her, Valerie thought that woman looked the same every time. They greeted each other kindly like they did every time, and everyone went their own way.

After the old woman entered her apartment, Valerie decided she could go around the rooms quickly and then move to the other wing to start her research and get to know the tenants better. Exactly one hour passed in doing all the rooms, dusting off the dust and cleaning the mirrors.

She didn't want Mrs Mackgraver to think she wasn't doing her job. When she finished the cleaning duties, she went straight to the other wing. Besides all 13 rooms, the house had long corridors with large wood panelling and a soft red carpet.

In the part where the tenants lived, the furniture definitely looked very comfortable and expensive. The walls were snow-white, the ceilings high and everything felt expensive. Valerie decided to meet with everyone under the pretext of offering cleaning services. Although it was not usual for many people to be home in the middle of the day, she still decided to try, hoping that at least one of them would have time for her.

She felt the thrill of this little investigation. When she was 11, she had decided to become a forensic scientist, maybe just for the thrill. As a child, she played such chase games, and that thrill could not be replaced by anything else. Over the years, her dreams changed, but they were always about investigation. When she was a teenager, she decided it was possible to become a police officer, but her romantic notions that she would be a protector of the world didn't cover reality.

Criminology could give her this opportunity through science. Now she saw that the knowledge she was getting at university could be put into practice this summer.

True, she didn't feel very prepared, but she wasn't convinced she'd have to investigate anything at all. After all, this was a slightly eccentric elderly woman who was alone, and nothing prevented her from parting with a few hundred quid a month, to pay for cleaning up her needlessly large home, which she still held, most likely out of sentimental inducements. In addition to her monthly income, this woman also received rent from each of her tenants.

After enjoying the comfort of the hallway, Valerie decided to find the salon, because surely there was a lounge with a library on this floor. Right in the middle of the hallway, she walked past an open door. She decided to peek inside.

In front of her was an amazing sight. The lounge was gingerbread in colour with huge curtains on the windows, a huge table, and two dirty, white armchairs with gold threads, a large library, a pool table, a poker table, several chairs and a green yellow sofa. The floor was covered with a thick red carpet, and huge chandelier hung from the ceiling.

For a moment, Valerie thought about how uncharacteristic the furniture seemed to be relative to her hostess's personality. For Valerie, Mrs Mackgraver was a petty and clueless, albeit meticulous old woman to the bone.

However, she decided to go in and take a closer look at the salon. She also wanted to see what books were on the library shelves. She was just going in when a man's figure appeared. The girl was just about to move but she almost immediately occupied herself.

"Good afternoon," Valerie Smith began, "I'm Mrs Mackgraver's assistant." She walked toward the man with her arm outstretched and a dazzling smile.

"It's nice to see a young woman in this house," the man replied. "I'm Osmond Bolton and I live in apartment four. It's on this side of the hallway through two doors."

"Oh, so there're flats in this wing?" the girl wondered.

"In fact, they were rooms, but because they were as huge as this salon, Mrs Mackgraver's father turned them into small apartments. So in this wing there are five small apartments and this lounge. They're all inhabited, and like I said, I'm in number four."

Valerie looked at Mr Bolton. For a moment, she thought Mother Nature really makes a joke with people sometimes.

Mr Osmond was a model of imperfection. His height was no more than 165cm, his abdomen and pelvis were the same in size, his shoulders were tight and his legs were flat like small sausages. He was wearing wide trousers, which were probably meant to hide away his imperfections in grey, and his body was covered in a shirt–which was probably left by his ancestors, faded and shrunk from the laundry. His slightly bald head had an egg shape, with a face untouched by the sun, a pebble nose, split brown eyes and thin lips. On top of his nose, he had placed glasses with very thin frames. Valerie would say that Mr Bolton was in his 50s. But the best thing about him was the timbre of his voice and his manners. He was deep and dense with impeccable upbringing. He uttered the words distinctly and very politely. And as Valerie soon found out, he was also a very good interlocutor. Mr Osmond continued his conversation with her.

"I'm very happy with your visit of whatever nature it is, seeing a young and beautiful person makes you feel better for a whole day."

"Oh, that's very sweet," Valerie smiled, "I actually wanted to see this part of the building and offer cleaning services. If you or your roommates need something like this, please let me know. Although I didn't ask the housekeeper, I decided to come and tell you anyway."

"Oh, don't worry, I won't betray you. Would it be irrelevant for you to tell me otherwise what do you do?"

"I'm a student at Durham University," Valerie began, and suddenly she realised how the words in that conversation were so subtle, and this gentleman's courtesy didn't fit his appearance at all. "I'm studying forensics and I just finished my freshman year," the girl continued.

"Interesting," Bolton said, "a pretty, beautiful, young lady who, after a while, will hold a gun and save the world."

"I don't think the world will be saved, but if I can help uncover some tangled case, it will help humanity."

"You really are an intelligent girl. And you managed to win me over on your side. I'd love for you to come clean once a week; what day can we do it?" asked Osmond.

"Let it be Tuesday," Valerie said, "anyway I'm coming here to Mrs Mackgraver's, it's going to be easier for me–once I'm done with her, to get up to you."

"Great," Bolton replied, "Tuesday is the perfect day for me. Look, I'm actually a statistician and I like my job. It could be a very good job for you one day when you start in the police, but my specialty is the census population and the total purchasing ability of the individual divided by age. We're doing research, tracking the statistics. The reason you find me here today is a lot of banal, pain in the back that won't let me move. I usually work Monday to Friday from 8 to 5, and this will give you the opportunity after you've finished on the board to get up here."

"Actually, I'm working till 4:00 pm."

"That's great; I'm going to be home at seven, so you're going to have plenty of time to do your job. I'll leave you the key right here," and Bolton showed off a can of sugar.

"Thank you for your trust," Valerie said, "I hope I can justify it."

"I hope so," the statistician replied, "but I dare say I have a flair for people."

She then decided to ask about the other occupants of the house, since he looked like the host of this part of the building.

"Can I ask you one more thing, Mr Bolton?"

"Let's not be so formal," Bolton interrupted her, "call me Osmond. But please say so?"

"Do I have any chance of offering the other occupants of the house my services? Can you tell me something about the people here?"

"I'll try to be as comprehensive as possible, and when I'm done, you can draw your own conclusions. I've lived here for twelve years. I came to Newcastle at the end of 2007 after being offered a job at the institute. Most roommates and I have been living as neighbours for years now. Only the woman in apartment No. 5 across the hall from mine has been here about a year. But let's sit down and I'll tell you about each individual."

They sat on the huge soft sofa. Mr Bolton offered coffee, which was received with gratitude by Valerie.

"So, let's start again with flat No. 1. It is located on the right side of the hallway, shortly after the door of the salon. It's where Edward lives and I remember his last name is Brighton Carmichael. He's 57 years old, divorced without children. He has lived in the house almost as long as I have. When he got here, he had just been divorced from his wife. He left her house to her and her two, royal poodle dogs. He claims that throughout his family-life, his wife cared for many more animals he watched and he never felt well there. He's a hopeless romantic, but his divorce has been well. Edward is a professor of literature at Newcastle University. He is extremely distracted and careless towards everything but his profession. He didn't ask for a lot of money with literature, and it ended up leaving him broke. Edward is a good friend of mine; we spend a lot of nights here playing cards and drinking sherry. Even though he's five years older, we have a full

19

understanding on a lot of issues. He's an intelligent man, but like I said, he's an incorrigible romantic."

"Do you think he'd get interested in cleaning the apartment?" involved Valerie.

"Why not? I can whisper to him, too. I've been into his apartment, and if you ask me, he's in great need of a woman's hand. Like I said, he's quite distracted and not strong in cleaning. Besides, I think he can pay for the favour. We both spend our money mostly on food, rent and sherry."

"I'd appreciate it if you'd ask him for me. I really need that money. And now is the time of vacation, time to make a little more money for next year, because then it's my practice and I'm going to have very little free time."

"This week around Friday, I'll see him and talk about your proposal. I'll do what I can."

"Thank you, Osmond, but I think I have taken a lot of your time today. I really have to go. I will count on you to convince your friend, and if not, I thank you in advance for the good attitude."

Valerie had already gotten up from the couch and reached out to Mr Osmond. When he got up to send her along, they both exchanged phone numbers.

It was 3.54 pm when Valerie arrived at her apartment. As she was walking home, she had tried to analyse the information Osmond Bolton had provided her. Despite some doubts Johnny had about the mystery of the house and the doubts that were raised by Mrs Mackgraver herself, Valerie saw almost nothing more than a large house with several occupants and a strange, elderly hostess.

She wished she could make Saturday come quicker to give Johnny the new information, but so far there were only two of the occupants who seemed to be just ordinary people. When she came home, she immediately looked at the electron clock on the wall. Sitting down at the kitchen table, she pulled out the diary she had been writing for several months and recorded:

3:54 pm Tuesday, 20 July 2017

I can't understand Johnny's desire in finding something wrong in Grove Village. The truth is, I wish something interesting happened to me too. Aside from university and regular outings with Johnny, nothing exciting happens to me. And I really want it to. The good thing is, I have a job, and now work is starting to increase. But to make it a little more exciting, I'm going to do our little investigation and try to get to know the residents there better by the end of the month. One of the things I learned in Dr Page's lectures was to be precise in recording the time of the event. This definitely reminds me quite often to write down my appointment and to monitor exactly what action I perform and when. So too, Mrs Mackgraver is meticulous and constantly monitors the hours, which is quite strange because at her age and in her nature of work, she hardly needs to be so accurate. I'm going to take a bath and I'm going to order a greasy takeaway and watch a movie.

Valerie performed exactly what she wrote. After taking a bath, she lay down for a while, and for dinner she ordered Chinese food, watched a movie and spent a quiet evening.

The next morning, she decided it was best to sit down and write the layout of the house, and also the description of

Edward and Osmond. She also decided to add Mrs Mackgraver. One of the things that brought her closer together to Johnny was that they both had a taste for adventure, but they had different points of view. And with two partners, Dr Page said, that was very important because they saw different things in the investigation. After she made her coffee, Valerie got some piece of paper and wrote about her encounter with Osmond Bolton, a man who was an absolute opposite of who he was on the outside. Despite the obvious ugliness, this man was so intelligent, he spoke with such aplomb that when the girl left she could not say a single simple word for hours.

Second, she wrote the story of the literature professor – the friend of Osmond Bolton.

Valerie stopped. Looking at the writing, she despaired, as she had nothing.

She got up, ripped the sheet, poured herself some more coffee, and decided to quit everything, at least for that day. She took a shower, got dressed and decided to take a walk outside. She went out on the main street and started staring at the shops. She wasn't thinking about buying anything at all, but she definitely had to let go of the pressure. She wanted to experience an exciting summer, not just pass the days till September. The question in her head was: how could this happen? She'd been walking the streets aimlessly for more than two hours and decided it was time to go home and eat something. On the way home, her phone rang.

"Hi Val," Johnny said.

"Hey, what's up?"

"Look, Val, I have a four-hour shift with the agency at Newcastle University on Friday. Because the event is big, the agency is looking for more people for waiters and bartenders.

From what I understand, it's going to be a faculty-only party, no students. We'll be done by 3:00 in the morning. Pay is minimal, but there may be tips."

"I don't know Johnny, it's not a job for me, and I don't have any experience," Valerie replied.

"Oh, Val, you don't need experience, you just need to carry a few plates, and you can get away with it at such big events. And at the end of the night, you'll get £100. Don't you get attracted to that?" Johnny asked.

"Honestly not. I'm working at Mrs Mackgraver on Friday, and then I'm going to have to work all night. No, Johnny, I'm not doing this. I will see you for breakfast Sunday."

"Okay, Val, I hope you'll have something to tell me."

"There are some things, but all this on Sunday. Bye."

"Bye, Val."

She unlocked the door and immediately went into the bathroom. She had to admit that she didn't expect the weather to be so warm for so many days in a row. Already on the fourth day, thermometers showed 25 degrees, and along with the humidity of the island, this definitely felt like much more.

It was very warm again at noon on Friday. Despite the heat, Valerie was again wearing the same suit and gloves and going to Grove Village. Along the way, she thought about the house mistress' little quirks about cleanliness and wearing these insane clothes. There was something puzzling about the woman's behaviour, but without ever speaking, she couldn't understand why she was doing this.

And all of a sudden, it occurred to her, well if she asked Osmond, he might know something about Mrs Mackgraver's past, he'd been in this house for 12 years and he must know something. She thought that when she got to work, she'd go and ask Osmond if he wasn't at work.

As always, the job was boring. Sometime after she did her chores, she went to the salon and waited for the hour to come for the lady to pay her. Once again, she looked at the library, there she saw a lot of books of law that probably belonged to Mr Mackgraver.

They probably haven't been touched for years, in this salon, it was like no one ever came down, Valerie thought.

To kill time, she decided to pick up *Anna Karenina* as she hadn't read these classic works yet. At home, she was always the 'little boy'. She grew up in a normal family with two normal parents, a rarity these days. She was an only child, but the upbringing her parents gave her was to deal with life as a man. They both wanted her to succeed more than they had.

Her mother was a nursery teacher and her father was a plumber. From an early age, she was getting more than they could give her. Her mother told her stories of brave girls who one day conquered the world. She was sure that her daughter was not born to be a princess, but rather to be a ruler. Somehow, between children's tales and her mother's bold tales of heroines, Valerie began reading mostly crime novels.

Sherlock Holmes was one of her favourite characters, she had read everything that had been released so far. She had a dream to go to London and look at his house there because she believed he really lived there. Edgar Allan Poe and Agatha Christie were also her favourites. So came her long-thought-out decision not to become a police officer, but a forensic scientist.

"Forensics had a more exciting daily routine," she said.

They were studying exactly what happens in crime, and they were also studying the psychology of the criminals. But somewhere between forensics and the upbringing of a *male* girl, there wasn't that typical girl romance in Valerie. So when she started *Anna Karenina* and wrapped herself up a passage of romantic character, she was amazed at how it was possible for the heroine to devote so much time to love's anguish.

As always, at 4:15 pm, the mistress of Grove Village welcomed her downstairs to pay her. They congratulated each other, Valerie got the money for a receipt and left.

When Mrs Mackgraver went to her flat, Valerie ran up the stairs. She went to the salon first to see if Mr Osmond Bolton was there by accident. When she didn't find him, she headed to his apartment. She knocked a few times, but no one answered. Apparently, he was at work. She didn't want to raise suspicion in the old lady's mind.

Just as she was leaving, she saw the door of an apartment open.

It was No. 5. She decided to knock and explain to the woman that she was cleaning and could help her if she needed it. She knocked a few times, and after no one called, she nudged the door. She looked around and didn't see anyone. Across the door were a countertop and a little kitchen. It was like a dollhouse. The pink colour prevailed everywhere; even the slippers by the door were pink. Valerie knocked on the door, which was probably the bedroom. Opening it, what she saw didn't surprise her. Everything inside was pink. Everything was so tidy and clean, she was only wondering why the door was open.

Valerie noticed a large portrait on the wall and approached to look at it. Even though she was a woman, she couldn't help but whistle with surprise when she looked at the photo. The woman in this picture was not more than 35 years old. Her raven-black hair flowed loosely over her shoulders, her face was round with grey-blue eyes, thick lips and a lovely straight nose. Valerie had never seen such a beautiful woman in her life. But there was something in her eyes that she couldn't help but say what it was, whether it was insidious or ironic. The photo was up to the waist, but judging by the structure, the woman was probably tall and slender.

"It's like she's perfect," the girl thought.

She decided that this woman probably wouldn't need her services. She came out slowly and just pulled the door behind her. When she left the house, she was still thinking about the enigmatic woman, wondering why she lived there and what she was dealing with. She was going to tell Johnny about her, because even though there was no mystery to solve, there were a lot of strange things in this house.

On Sunday at 11 am, both Valerie and Johnny were punctual and arrived at the same time at the café for brunch.

"I have so much to tell," Valerie began enthusiastically.

"Then you go first," Johnny replied.

"Okay, Joe, sit down and let's not forget this breakfast is on you today."

"You got it."

When they settled in and ordered the coffee and waffles with lots of chocolate, Valerie unfolded her diary and started from scratch.

"I guess I wrote to you that I met one of the occupants in the house, and it was by accident. He turned out to be a very nice middle-aged man. He's friends with a professor at the university. Of course, I offered them cleaning services because I couldn't explain my attendance there."

"The ball I was at yesterday," Johnny interrupted her, "it was just for teachers. I wonder if he was there."

"I haven't seen him in person, but I can tell you what Osmund told me about him Johnny, but I don't think you've been looking around all night to see exactly this English literature professor."

"You're right, to tell you the truth," the boy replied. "When you're serving at a party like this, you don't have much time to look around the visitors. Val?"

"To be honest, I was interested in talking to Mr Osmund. Johnny, you can't imagine what a contradiction there is between his appearance and his manners. It's so weird, he's a very disproportionate man, but he speaks so politely."

"Does he teach at the university?" asked Joe.

"No, no, he's a statistician; his friend in the apartment next door is the teacher."

While they were talking, Johnny gave the waiter a sign and ordered two more coffees and one orange juice. Valerie continued the conversation after sipping the coffee.

"But let's put these two aside. On Friday, while I was at work," Valerie started again, "something very interesting happened. I had decided to go upstairs to look for Mr Osmond Bolton, but he wasn't there. Then I saw the door of one of the apartments open and after making sure there was no one, I went inside. Inside, I saw a portrait of one of the most beautiful women you can imagine. I couldn't find a speck. After I walked around the door, I left."

"Wow," exclaimed Johnny, "didn't you have the thought of digging?"

"No, I wasn't comfortable, what if someone came in at that moment?"

"Well, it would have been exciting for me."

"Oh, Joe, I can't risk my job and reputation and be accused of negligence."

"Yes, but you could still find out what her name is?"

"I could have, but I didn't dare. Tell me now how the ball was and do you find the new job interesting?" asked Valerie in turn.

"Oh, Val, I'm just serving plates first. Second, we bring the drinks, and then we serve. Val you know we are working those jobs because we need to pay the bills but our dream is different."

"I know, but we can't get there this fast."

They had already finished with the second coffee; the brunch was already going through an afternoon snack, so they both decided to get up.

"When am I going to see you again?" asked Valerie.

"It's been a busy week for me, there are a lot of weddings and I'm going to have to work. But I'll probably be free on Sunday."

"All right, let's have it again Sunday," Valerie agreed, "but this time at home. I'll try to make something delicious to eat."

"I hope this summer will be really exciting."

"I believe that."

They split up in front of the place. On the way to her home, Valerie's phone rang.

"Hi Valerie," Osmond Bolton began, "I was wondering if you remember our conversation about cleaning the apartment?"

"Of course Osmond, I remember."

"Then let's work out and see you, I'll show you exactly what I want from you. When you get here, we'll sort out the money. Do you agree?"

"Yes, it's okay. If you want, I can work on Tuesday after I'm done with Mrs Mackgraver."

"Unfortunately, I won't be able to meet you at this time. But if you're free on a Saturday at 10:00 am, I could invite you to the salon and introduce you to all the occupants of the house. As far as I know, you don't know anyone else."

At one point, Valerie thought about telling him she was already in one of the apartments, but immediately decided it wasn't a good idea, as he could accuse her of stealing or something else.

"Yes," Valerie said, "it would be great to meet everybody."

"Great, let's do it Saturday at 10:00 am. I'm going to make you the best coffee, and you're going to feel really hospitable with us. We're a big family here."

"Thank you, Mr Bolton, sorry, Osmond," Valerie said. "Goodbye, see you Saturday."

"See you on Saturday, Valerie."

When she hung up the phone, Valerie wondered if she'd see the woman whose photo she saw on the wall. She thought she'd know when she went to Grove Village. Summer didn't come out so boring after all; at least there would be a proper job.

On Saturday, Valerie got up early, as she wanted to work out before she went to the house. At 6 am, it was already bright outside, but there were no people. She went to the park to run and then went home to finish the workout in her small apartment. She had a whole room to exercise she had bought resistance bands and dumbbells. She managed to train for an hour, then went into the bathroom, changed her clothes and sat down to drink coffee. Today, she was about to make a deal with Osmond for cleaning, she was going to become more stable financially.

For her, all this was good. She was going to buy some interesting things. For one, criminologist-like dust for making fingerprints, a more powerful computer, and special gloves. If criminology was what she was going to do for a living, she wanted to put her money there now.

When she finished her coffee and the list of things to buy, she put on trousers and a short-sleeved shirt, put on her beautiful, floral sandals and headed for the house. She had decided that she didn't want to alert Mrs Mackgraver, so she was going to go through the other entrance, where the tenants were probably coming in. Before she went upstairs, she breathed a deep breath. Although she wasn't bothered, there was a slight nervousness before she walked in through the door. She knocked and almost immediately, Osmond Bolton opened the door.

"Hi, Valerie, I'm glad you came. Please come in," he introduced her to the salon.

"Hi Osmond, good to see you again" she held out her hand to him.

"I'll show you all people here and introduce them to you. Now let me get the coffee and we'll work things out about cleaning my apartment. As we discussed, it's only going to be a week on Tuesdays when Mrs Mackgraver's work ends, I'll give you a key to come here." Osmond continued, "I don't think we're going to take you for more than two hours, that's until about 6:00. I'm not going to be home at this hour, but I'm going to leave your money on the kitchen table. Do you think these conditions suit you, Valerie?"

"You know I'm a student, and I need that income, even though they don't develop my skills as a forensic scientist."

"Valerie, you're still very young, you have time to gain experience. Oh my God, I forgot about the coffee."

He walked to the kitchen quickly and at the door came literature professor Edward Brighton. Valerie got up from the couch to say hello.

She was way taller than him, she noticed. The professor was small, with loose hair, scattered, or rather not combed properly. He had warm brown eyes, thick-rimmed glasses, a small nose and thin lips. His face was wrinkled, but in general he seemed like a good man. His jacket and trousers were at least two numbers larger.

When she saw it, Valerie immediately thought of that inevitable pattern that the smarter you are, the more careless you are about your looks. As they exchanged pleasantries, Osmond Bolton was already coming in with the coffee.

"Ed, that's the girl I was talking about," Bolton began.

"Yes, we just met, Oz," the professor said. "I'd really like to help you, but I really don't need cleaning up."

"But how Ed, your room looks like it has been through a tornado," Bolton interrupted him.

"I'm so pleased with this mess, and most of all, no one's going to get involved in it. I'm sorry, sweet girl."

"Oh, don't worry, I already have enough work for the summer. And from September, I won't have that much time anyway," Valerie replied.

"Yes, Osmond told me you're studying forensics in Durham. I love this city, there's something magical about it with its narrow streets and quaint buildings."

"Have you been to the festival of lights?" asked Valerie.

"No, but I can visit it in the winter."

"I was there last year and I was very impressed. After you go all over the city and see all the lights on the buildings, stop in front of the cathedral there, they do a show with sound and it is magical. It's like they're carrying you into antiquity and you feel that time with all its positives and negatives. The atmosphere they create is really fascinating."

"I'm going to go, for sure," the professor replied, "you have really intrigued me."

"I think it's time to hold on to a lot of tear-jerkers."

"Oh, you were very nice company," Osmond interjected. "I guess I won't be able to introduce you to the others, but I might tell you about them and ask them on your behalf."

"Of course," Valerie agreed.

"What are you going to tell the girl about the tenants of the house, Osmond? There is Marius's gardener, who I think is from Southern Italy, and Oliver Grundy, an assistant professor of chemistry at my university."

"You're going to forget somebody," Osmond said, "what about the girl from No 5?"

"Oh, yes, I totally forgot it. Maybe it's because I haven't seen her in a long time."

"I haven't spoken to her in a while, and she's my neighbour. Do you want to go see if she's there?"

"I'm going to go with you," Valerie said, "and then I'm really going to go."

Osmond Bolton and Valerie left the salon, and the professor stayed to finish his coffee. They went out into the hallway and rushed to the apartment. When they got to the door, Valerie noticed it wasn't open now. Osmond knocked hard, but no sound was heard from the inside, waited a little and knocked a second time. With a strong push, the door opened.

"Damn," he said, "it looks like the door is open."

He nudged her and went inside. Out of curiosity, Valerie followed him. It was neat and clean inside, as if nothing had been touched.

"You know," Osmond started, "this is Miss Amalie Druster's apartment. She's been here a while, but as far as I know, she's not such a good housewife. It's like everything's too tidy."

"Osmond," Valerie started, "can I tell you something that's very strange, but I can't hide it?"

"Of course," he replied.

The two were standing inside of the door.

"On Tuesday," the girl continued, "After I was done with Mrs Mackgraver, I decided to go up and look for you so I could be aware of your cleaning plans. I knocked on your door, but no one answered. At that moment, it occurred to me to ask the other occupants of the house. The door of this apartment was open and I decided to ask here too. No one answered, I walked in and called, but no one called back. Then I didn't stick and went into the bedroom. And there, from a portrait, I was looking at the most beautiful woman I've ever seen. I admired the portrait, and on the way out, I must have opened the door more."

"Do you think for five days, no one noticed that the door was open?" Osmond asked.

"I have no idea," Valerie said, "but nothing seems to have been touched. I have a photographic memory, Mr Bolton, sorry, Osmond, and I remember everything was in the same place as today."

"There must be something wrong. I suggest we call the police department and alert the inspector."

Valerie jumped in for joy, but refrained from shouting.

"Do you think I could stay?" she asked.

"Of course, you might be helpful. After all, you say everything is the same as before, it would be good to confirm it to the officer."

"Oh, thank you very much, I will finally have the opportunity to apply what I have learned, or at least follow the process."

"I know the inspector. Let me just find the phone and I'll make a call."

Mr Bolton went to his apartment and returned with two big books like guides. Valerie followed him with a look at how he opened the pages, and they were all numbered in alphabetical order.

He was an orderly person, she noted. He went for the letter K and dialled a number.

"Hi, Inspector Karston, this is Osmond Bolton of Grove Village. I wouldn't bother you, but something strange is happening here at our boarding house."

Bolton described exactly how they found Amalie's apartment and also mentioned Valerie and the open door. When he hung up the phone, he told Valerie that the inspector would be here within the hour to talk. Bolton took his notebooks and he and Valerie moved into the salon, where they would tell the inspector about their discovery. Lunch was already approaching, and Osmond and the professor decided to offer lunch to the girl.

As the quickest option, they ordered Indian food from the nearest Indian restaurant. Valerie was amazed by the taste, as she had never tasted such food before. After lunch, Osmond made more coffee and waited for the inspector. Valerie had already sent a message to Johnny saying she had a lot to tell him on Sunday. She felt very excited. She had never been to a crime scene before. Of course, this could have been the most ordinary negligence on the part of the lady, but it could also have been something deeper.

It was almost two hours before someone knocked at the door. It'd been more than two hours since Osmond called the inspector. A young man came into the salon. Detective Inspector Josh Karston, 33, had been a police officer for 10 years. He had walked all the floors of the service and, on his own merits, had risen to an inspector. He was a tall, muscular and handsome young man. He had black hair, brown eyes and thick lips. His face was matte, he had a high forehead, and when he spoke, his white teeth were revealed.

A well-groomed man, his life's dream was to become a police officer. And it was already a dream that had come true. In all 10 years of his service after graduating from the police school, he had not faced many interesting criminal cases.

On one hand, Newcastle was a provincial city with a hardly exciting crime scene. On the other hand, people lived well economically and didn't have to perform crimes to survive. Before he became a cop, Karston dreamed of this job and was looking forward to a very exciting future, but the reality was a little different.

Over the years working in the police force as a naïve dreamer, Inspector Karston had become a slightly sceptical man who no longer trusted people so much and loved checking minuscule things about daily situations.

When he walked into the salon, he greeted the people inside and sat on one of the proposed chairs, pulled out his notebook and engaged in the conversation about the bizarre Amalie Druster case.

"All right, Mr Bolton, tell me what the problem is and what you know so far."

"Please call me Osmond," Bolton said. "The truth is, I had no idea until a while ago, but Valerie said that as early as Tuesday, she noticed that the door had been opened and there was no one inside."

"All right, Osmond," Josh Karston interrupted, "let's start over, I'd like to hear the lady and then tell you about it. Tell me, miss, what happened at the beginning of the week, but maybe first I'd like to know who you are and what are you doing here?"

"Well, my name is actually Valerie Smith and I'm studying forensics," the girl proudly remarked. "The truth is, I'm cleaning the house, and I went up to look for Mr Bolton on Tuesday. Because I didn't find it, I decided to ask if anyone else needed cleaning, when I approached I saw the door open, knocked, but no one answered me, so I walked in. There was nothing strange about it, there was no one, but it made the impression that it was impeccably clean."

"I'm going to ask you if there was anything strange about the door. Did you see any unusual prints," the inspector asked.

"No, there was nothing, Inspector. The only thing that impressed me was that today when we walked in with Mr Osmond, it was just as clean as it was on Tuesday," Valerie said.

"I get it. Let's go look together and I'll try to write the report. Mr Osmond, it would be nice if you tell me about the woman who lives in this apartment."

All three got up and went to apartment No. 5 to look around. The inspector came in alone to examine, and Valerie and Osmond waited outside. When he went to Amalie's bedroom, the inspector was awe-struck. He saw the woman's portrait and he was really stunned at the beauty. He then looked around and came out.

"Now, let's go to the salon again and I'm going to ask you to tell me about this woman, Amalie Druster," the inspector began.

"I'd like to tell you a lot of things, but I can't," Osmond began, "Miss Amalie Druster moved into Grove Village no more than a year ago. As you may have seen from her portrait, she's a very beautiful woman. Because mostly men live here, you can imagine our happiness when Amalie showed up. As far as I know, she is currently working as a kindergarten assistant teacher. She's been working for a while. Besides being beautiful, she's also very funny. We have had a couple of well-spent nights here in the salon, but that's it."

"We all noticed that it was very clean in her apartment, do you think she's a good hostess?" the inspector asked again.

"No, I do not think so," Osmond replied. "At the times we've met, she's not very keen to help with the cleaning, but who knows, maybe there's a different one in her house."

"Do you know if she happens to have a lot of visitors?" the inspector asked again.

"Honestly, I haven't seen anyone come here. But keep in mind that I work every day from Monday to Friday all day, and in that time someone may have visited her."

"You, Valerie," the officer turned to the girl, "what do you know about Miss Amalie?"

"Inspector Karston, I've never seen her, I told you what I found, I guess that's all," Valerie said.

"We really don't know her well, no one's been following her and calling her, and she might have just gone out and gone somewhere."

"Yes," the inspector said, "it's possible, but it's unlikely. I'm concerned that I'm going to contact her relatives and continue the investigation."

"Could I be of any use to you?"

"Look, Valerie, I can't officially include you, but you can help me as you come here so often. But before I leave, I want to tell you if there's anything, just call me."

The inspector spun on his heels and with a theatrical gesture, walked out of the salon.

"I think its best that Mrs Mackgraver doesn't know about it. Maybe nothing happened anyway, and there's no point in bothering her."

"I agree," Valerie confirmed.

"It's okay with me," the professor said, "I'm out of here a lot, and I rarely see her."

It was afternoon now, and Valerie finally decided to leave.

"Thank you, Professor, for your pleasant company and to you, Osmond, for everything, I'll see you on Tuesday."

"I'll leave you the key, as we agreed," Osmond said goodbye.

Valerie got out quickly and headed for the street. She was sure something was happening and that made her happy. There was hope that summer would not be boring. She couldn't wait to tell Johnny tomorrow. She went through a store to shop for tomorrow's brunch. She came home and decided she could watch movies all night and eat chocolate.

When she woke up in the morning, her entire sheet was covered in chocolate. As an exemplary cleaner and a forensic scientist, he thought she might wait for the cleaning. So she put the coffee on the stove and waited for Johnny to come.

"You know, Joe, I think I'm getting interested in Grove Village," Val said.

It was 11 am, and Johnny was at the kitchen table.

"Tell me everything."

"So," said Valerie mysteriously, "I'd already told you about that beautiful woman in the portrait I saw in the house. Turns out she's been missing for a week. Because the lodgers were worried that the door had been opened, a police inspector was called."

"Oh, you see Val, interesting days are coming," Johnny said.

"I don't know, she might just be out, even though it looks pretty unusual. Inspector Josh Karston questioned us, and it was kind of very exciting for me. We didn't take any prints, but it was flawlessly clean."

"Okay, so if there's anything, you'll tell me. Now let me tell you what happened to me. It's not that exciting, but you can find it interesting."

"Is there something interesting in your love life, my friend?" asked Valerie.

"Oh, honey, you know I don't care about anyone at this point. Besides, if that happens, you'll be the first to know," he replied.

"I know, I know, Johnny. Well. Tell me what's in it," she asked with curiosity.

"Remember that shift you got in the university banquet hall?"

"Yes, we didn't see each other for some time, right?"

"That's when we worked with two other guys my age. We were a team. Let me explain to you, at such big events, we are assigned by teams, figuratively speaking, and so we serve a large area of tables. So, the other day, we were waiters at an Indian wedding. We served a lot of people. We were assigned five people per team and we fell together again. So between the main dish and dessert we had a break of 20 minutes. We had a quick meal and went to smoke a cigarette outside. We talked about the university, and then Mark, with great excitement, said that last time he served some woman who was extremely beautiful."

"Wow, are you saying this is Amalie Druster from Grove Village?"

"It's possible because he said all the boys talked about her. She had black long hair, tall and slender."

"Oh, you know who she was with?" asked Val.

"I have no idea," Johnny replied, "but I can ask the guys during the week."

"That'll help me. Ask them, that's valuable information."

"I'll do it."

"Now let's focus on the food, Val, and go for a walk after this job, so we don't have time for anything else."

"I'm not complaining, Joe," Valerie said with a smile.

After they ate, they went for a walk on the main one. The summer in northern England was surprisingly behaving very decently. It hadn't rained for three weeks and the temperatures were feeling quite summery. When they went outside, they both decided that the best walk would be on the beach.

For Valerie, the sea was the beauty she needed. Although it was much colder in Newcastle, the beauty of the endless expanse was something few people could resist.

"Val, let's take my car and show you a very beautiful place," John said.

"Okay, just let's go somewhere and get a cup of coffee," Valerie replied.

"No, you don't have to, there's everything there. It's close and very beautiful."

"We're going then," Valerie said.

It'd been no more than half an hour when they made it to Marsden Beach, a place Johnny had discovered a long time ago, a little, rocky beauty. Valerie thought there were really a lot of beautiful places in England. The sun was already low and shining even stronger. In the summer, it was bright until very late. After walking along the rocks, which were very densely to the shore they had formed something like caves and in some places it was really steep.

After this difficult but satisfying walk, Johnny took her to the beachfront pub. It was carved into the rocks and inside it had a rather muted light. It was really very interesting, so they decided to finish the afternoon in a typically English way – with afternoon tea. Tea was Valerie's favourite drink, and served like this, with sweets and small sandwiches, it felt gorgeous.

Valerie came home in the evening and read some of the forensics book before she fell asleep.

Next week, everything started perfectly normally. On Tuesday, Valerie went to work and when she finished Mrs Mackgraver's part she came to Osmond's floor. They had arranged to leave her the key in the salon in a small sugar can. Valerie found it and went to unlock apartment No. Four.

After she went inside, Valerie looked around. The apartment was furnished with taste, not unlike the rest of the house. The apartment had a bedroom, a living room and a small kitchenette. The bathroom was small, but cosy and with a bathtub.

Mr Osmond Bolton didn't seem like an orderly man, but he definitely maintained his place. Even though she wanted to know more about his life, Valerie didn't want to go through his stuff. He was always nice to her. Polite and thoughtful, he has always been well-intentioned. It was as if he was helping her now, as apparently he didn't need much of her services. Valerie handled it for about an hour, locked the door behind her and went to the salon to leave the key. When she got home, it was about seven o'clock. The sun was already hiding behind the horizon. Valerie wanted to rest as there were at least two outings at the end of the week. By 8:00 pm, she was ready for her dinner, and she sat down to enjoy it. At 8:45 pm, her phone started ringing. After the third call, she finally picked it up.

"Hello, Mr Osmond," she cheerfully greeted him.

"Hi, dear Valerie," he began, "look, I'm sorry to bother you, but here in Grove Village something happened, and you're going to have to come too."

"Ok, Osmond, should I come now, what happened?" the girl asked.

"Take a cab so I don't have to worry about you, but you don't have to rush. We'll wait for you here, since I'm not comfortable telling you on the phone."

"I'll be with you in 30 minutes."

When she started getting ready, Valerie wondered what might be so important that she had been called to the house at night, but she decided it was best to go and check on the spot. She called a cab and exactly 25 minutes after the call, she was outside the house. After ringing the doorbell, she wondered how Mrs Mackgraver would react. In her life everything was so drawn in minutes that ringing the door at 9:20 pm in the evening atypical, even indecent.

"Hey, Valerie," the inspector said, "come in, we're all gathered in the other wing, so we didn't hear you right away."

"Hi, Inspector," Valerie replied, "What happened? It's not typical for Mrs Mackgraver to welcome guests at this time."

"Yes, that's why we called you. Mrs Mackgraver is missing."

Valerie looked at the inspector.

"Well, obviously she's out this afternoon and hasn't come back until now, so we wanted to talk to everyone she's been communicating with today, so we can try to find her, and because you were here today, we had to call you."

As they spoke, they had imperceptibly made it to the large salon where all the roommates had gathered. Valerie wished everyone a good evening and sat on one of the high chairs at the table. Although she was worried, she also felt a little excited.

Everyone was gathered at the table. She first saw the gardener and chemistry assistant Oliver. It wasn't too hard to tell one from the other. Marius, the gardener, was a light tanned, muscular and well-placed man. He had Asian features: big black eyes, plump lips and a straight nose. Like any young man, he looked at her from the bottom-up, with a keen look. He had a bit of a frivolous look and Valerie definitely didn't like it, although he was pretty confident.

In contrast, the assistant Oliver Grandy was still young, and wore thick-rimmed glasses. He was skinny and tall with a small nose, thin lips and small eyes. His skin was transparently white. You could tell he didn't show up much outside. After everyone settled in, the inspector started.

"I guess you know why we're here today. Mr Osmond Bolton called me that Mrs Mackgraver was missing. From what I understand, it's not common for her to go out after 6:00 pm in the evening, so we're worried she's gone. She didn't come home, nor did she call. I would ask anyone with any information to share it so we can do an investigation and find Mrs Mackgraver. Tell me, Mr Bolton, why did you go to the missis's apartment?"

"Let me first point out that Mrs Mackgraver and I meet one single time in the month when I pay her rent. Since she is no longer of age and I can't or won't transfer it by bank transfer, on the 10th of each month, at 9:00 am in the morning, I call and give her the cheque. Today's extraordinary visit was to warn her that a colleague of mine from university was going to visit me in a week. I just wanted to tell her about this visit. When I got there, the door was open, I knocked, but because no one answered, I went inside. I looked everywhere for her, there was no one. I waited a while and no one showed

44

up. I went up to my apartment and decided to look for her a little later. After about two hours I tried again, but there was no one there this time either. Everything was like I found it the previous time. I looked at the clock and saw that it was 8 pm. Since it is very unusual for her to be gone, I just called you, Inspector."

"Yes, the truth is, we're still hoping she is coming back. But because it's too late now, we are starting to ask everybody."

"Tell me, Valerie, did she tell you something?"

"Oh, Inspector, I'm sorry to disappoint you, but Mrs Mackgraver and I almost never talk. Our only talks are on Friday, when she pays my wages for the week. In the meantime, we greet each other, and that's it. Mrs Mackgraver is a woman who likes accuracy, and only minimal deviation can get her out of control."

"I understand Valerie, so you can't help us," the frustrated inspector replied. "Did any of you communicate with the lady recently?" he addressed the attendees.

They all shook their heads.

Gardener Marius called, "Well, I'm not talking to the missis. She's not much of a talker. But she pays well."

"Okay, so I have to get on with the investigation," said Inspector Karston, on his way to the door.

Valerie jumped up and caught up with him at the door.

"You know, I'm studying forensics, I'm going to practice with you next year, but now a case has come out and I could be of use to you."

"I'm not sure it's a good idea, although maybe I'd need some help. I'm sure I'm going to have to search her apartment."

"I could be of use to you. That way I can learn new things. I'm going to put in the paperwork for practicing with you. Please, Inspector," called Valerie.

The girl is really beautiful and I need an extra person, so why not, Karston thought.

"All right," he said, "only you're going to do what I tell you, no teenage stupidity."

"Yes, Sir," said Valerie, with respect.

"Well then," Karston said, "our first job is to get downstairs and take a look around the lady's apartment."

The two of them went down the stairs, and Valerie decided to thank him for the chance he gave her.

"I'm really reading a lot this summer on the subjects I need for the next year. I promise I'll help you. I'll try to remind myself exactly what I need to look at when I look."

"Okay, Valerie, I'm doing this because I was just like you before. I'm glad you want to make progress. Let's get to the apartment now. I guess you've been here before, and you know the location."

"Actually, Inspector, she never let me in, so I'd be interested to see what it is."

"I know she's a really weird woman."

"A lot."

When they came down, the apartment door was still open. It was particularly interesting for Valerie to go inside and look at the apartment of the woman she had worked for the last year. For Inspector Karston, it was just a job. He opened the door wide and went inside, followed by the girl.

Mrs Mackgraver's flat was very spacious. It started with a huge hallway, followed by three huge bedrooms, a living room and a kitchen. It had high ceilings and didn't look like any of the other apartments in Grove Village. The furniture was minimalist and everything was well chosen, in every corner they could see how well maintained everything was. There was no dust or rubbish anywhere.

"All right, Valerie," the inspector said, "we're going to have a lot of work to do. Here's the plan, I'll start at this bedroom, and you go to the next one. As you can see, she's a meticulous woman, so if you find something unusual, just take it."

"Well, Inspector, I'm going to watch very carefully," Valerie replied.

They both went to the rooms, and Valerie wondered why this single woman needed such a huge home. Although the apartment itself looked very good, it was not yet known which one was the lady's bedroom. Valerie started her investigation carefully. She looked at the bedside tables, then the bed and the section, looked everywhere it was possible to hide something, but found nothing.

The inspector was also unsuccessful. They both moved on to the next room. It was about midnight, they were in the apartment for two hours, but the search didn't work and fatigue started saying its word. Then the inspector decided that it was best to finish for today and continue in the morning.

"Inspector, I'm obviously not going to have a job, since the missis is gone, could I continue the investigation with you? My summer is free anyway."

"I'll let you accompany me, and if you remember something unusual said or done by Mrs Mackgraver, it would be of great help."

"I'll think," Valerie said with a happy voice.

They were both preparing to leave. When he leaned under the shoe cabinet, he saw a piece of paper. He pulled it out and saw it was a bus ticket. The destination was Newcastle to Chester-Le-Street and back. The date was of today, 1 August 2017. The ticket was purchased that morning.

"I guess Mrs Mackgraver was on a walk today, if this trip had anything to do with her disappearance."

"I don't know, sir, it's possible, and what are we going to do now?"

"I'd like to think about it, and I'll call you in the morning. It's too late now, and I'm tired. Let's go. I'll get the ticket. Wait till 9:00 am tomorrow and I will tell you."

"I see, sir."

"And don't call me sir; Josh will be better. We'll work together."

"Ok, Josh."

After they got out of Grove Village, Valerie called a cab and went home.

The phone rang, it was exactly 9:00 am. Despite her great desire to get up early, she was still in bed.

"Hi Valerie," the inspector said, "I hope I didn't wake you up."

"Oh, no," the girl lied, "I've long been waiting for you to call me."

"Great, so in about 30 minutes, you should be ready to be picked up."

"Yes, where are we going," Valerie asked.

"We're going to Chester Le Street. It's not too far from here, and we should definitely check what Mrs Mackgraver was doing there."

"I'll be ready in half an hour."

"I'll meet you out front at 9:40 am."

"See you then."

After hanging up the phone, Valerie jumped out of bed and went to make coffee. At 9:40 am she was down in front of her block. Mrs Mackgraver had definitely taught her punctuality.

"You know," Inspector Karston began, "it was Tuesday. I checked and found out that in Chester Le Street every Tuesday, Thursday and Saturday there is a market. It's possible Mrs Mackgraver went there because of this market."

By the time he spoke, Inspector Josh Karston had already turned on the engine.

"How far is it, Inspector?"

"It won't take us more than 20 minutes. Because it's a small town, we'll be able to learn some things from the locals. They may have seen her. We'll ask."

"Can we get a cup of coffee first?"

"It works," Josh said, "and I'm going to buy breakfast because you're out of a job for now."

"Yes, Sir," Valerie said, laughing.

Karston just gave her a chilling look.

The road didn't take them long. Just 20 minutes later they were in town. As they travelled, the inspector questioned her about the university, and what she was actually studying.

"In general," Valerie began, "we've been studying mostly theory this year. For the history of forensics and for criminal law. Next year will definitely be more interesting to me because the practice begins. It would be great to be sent to work with you practically."

"Is there a possibility?" the inspector looked at.

"Yes, I think it's up to the professor. It's going to be great," Valerie replied.

"You're already practicing anyway," he replied.

"Yes, but if it's official, it'll be better. I wish I could handle real cases." Valerie said.

"Oh, what is that for you?" Karston asked.

"Well, I still think it's some kind of joke."

"I don't think the disappearance of a 70-year-old woman is a joke. Trust me, this is really serious."

"Maybe you're right, Inspector, I'm sorry," the girl said.

"We're here finally, I shall park here and we'll go ask the market."

"Great, come on," Val enthuses.

The two of them headed to the market. Chester Le Street wasn't such a small town. It was in County Durham, with greenery that was inherent in the whole of England, and brick houses and narrow streets that embody the serenity of English culture. On the days when there was a market, the town was visited by many people from nearby towns and villages. Everything from clothes to homemade meals could be found here. Valerie and Inspector Karston went that way. The market wasn't working today, but there were some of the people who were preparing for Friday's market. Inspector Karston headed towards a group of people who had stood right at the entrance to the market.

"Good morning," he greeted them, "I'm here with my assistant Valerie Smith. We're interested in any of you if they were in the market on Tuesday."

"Yes," answered a fat red-skinned man. "I sell at this stall right by the door. My name is Carl, and I've been here 30 years."

"Great," the inspector said, "can I ask you if you noticed a small, thin white-haired woman yesterday?"

"It's very difficult to say " Karl said, "yesterday the customers weren't many, and most were elderly. On Tuesday, mostly elderly people shop as the young are at work. Fridays and Saturdays are a different type of people. So I didn't see her."

"Thanks anyway," Karston replied. "Do you know where else I can ask?"

"Why don't you ask the market security, they'll know best."

"Thank you, Carl, I'm going to see them."

He and Valerie headed to security. They stopped in front of a cubicle and the inspector knocked on the door.

"Good morning, what do you love?" began the conversation with a white-haired man with a strict broadcast.

"Good morning," Karston said, "I'm an inspector from the police department. We were wondering if you could give us any information about a woman who should have been passing by yesterday. Small, thin, and white-haired."

"I'm going to need a more detailed description, since on Tuesday, most of our clients respond to that description."

At that point, Valerie stepped forward and described Mrs Mackgraver down to the slightest detail.

"Also," she continued, "just yesterday morning, she was wearing a grey skirt, a floral blouse and black shoes."

"That's something else now, honey," the security guard said. "The thing is, there was just that woman here, but she hadn't come to the market, and she came to us to ask us where the way to San Mary and St. Cuthbert's Church."

"What was it for her to know the way to the church?" the inspector asked. "Did she say anything more?"

"No, the only thing she asked was how to get there," the security guard replied.

"And at this time of year, are there any events that would take her there?" said Valerie.

"The girl's asking very specific questions, Inspector, it's a good thing you took her with you."

"We don't have events like that this summer, miss. There is a festival that is not only connected to our city, but it is held in the winter months and is not connected to the church, but to the creative schools, so I cannot tell you what you would do in the cathedral. But that should not prevent you from going to ask Father Edward, he is a good man will certainly respond and give you information."

Valerie and the inspector thanked the security guards and headed to the church to see if Mrs Mackgraver had been there. Saint Mary and St Cuthbert was a tall stone building built in the early 11th century. The tower of the church was very high. When they went inside, the lunch service had just finished, and the people had gone.

Valerie found a door and she knocked on it. Inside, a tall man was shown dressed all in black with a snowy white collar. His hair was already grey, his face sloping, with blue eyes, a wide forehead and well-formed lips. His nose was sharp, but straight. His whole being radiated kindness. His physique was pretty weak.

"Good afternoon," the inspector began. "I'd like to ask you a few questions. Could you give us a few minutes?"

"Of course," the father said, "I'm Father Edward, please come in. Let me make some tea and I'll pay attention to you."

"Great," the inspector said, "thank you."

When the father brought in the three cups of tea, Valerie and the inspector had already settled against each other at the big table.

"I'm listening to you, what's this about," the father asked.

"Valerie's my assistant, but until recently, she was working for Mrs Mackgraver. She's a 72-year-old woman who we assumed has been missing since before noon yesterday. We found a ticket to your town at her house, and because it was Tuesday, we assumed she went to the market. We were there a while ago, and they sent us to you from there. Since Mrs Mackgraver asked about the way to your church, did she come here, Father Edward?"

"Actually, yesterday morning, I really had a visitor. But after an hour, she left because I couldn't answer the questions she asked me. I told her to check on her, so we broke down next week to come and talk to me."

"May I ask you what questions she asked you and why you couldn't answer her right away?" the officer asked.

"I don't know if it's right for me to tell you the secrets of the people who come to me."

"I don't think her secret is that important if anything happens to her."

"You're right, Inspector, all right. When she came in yesterday morning, she asked me about a case happened 50 years ago. I told her I couldn't answer her because I didn't serve in the church at the time, but I promised her to check the records."

"What was it about," the inspector asked again. "What's the big deal?"

"Mrs Mackgraver came to ask me about some boy's christening."

"Did she mention his name?"

"Actually, yes, his name is Mark Sutton, or so it was recorded at the time. It happened in 1963. Since our church was built, we have kept an archive in which the name of every child who is baptised here is recorded. However, she did not know what month it was and this definitely makes the situation difficult, because I have to check every single page and every single sheet of the archive book."

"All right," the inspector said. "Did she tell you who this child is and why she cares about his baptism?"

"She said she'd trust me with some information after we found the date. She also said she would make a big donation to our church."

"Thank you, Father. Do you think we'll be able to get this information soon? It can help us in the search."

"I can get you the information," Father Edward said, "but I need at least two days."

"Well, Father, we'll be back on Friday if we haven't found anything new by then. Is it possible to ask any of the older parishioners about Mrs Mackgraver or the child she is looking for, who is probably now in his 50s."

"I could ask one of the older occupants tomorrow morning at 10:00 am. It's very likely that they know something."

"I'd appreciate it. And if there's anything urgent you want to tell me, here's my phone number."

Valerie had been following the conversation all along, she was reflecting on the information the father had given them, but nothing substantial had come up. When the inspector got up and gave the father a hand, Valerie got up, got out of the

54

church and went to the car. The afternoon was already raining and the two were hungry, the inspector suggested they sit in one of the small cafés on the main one for a quick lunch and then head to Newcastle.

"Are you sure Mrs Mackgraver doesn't have children?" asked Josh after they had settled in and were waiting for lunch.

"Yes, she's been living alone for years," Valerie replied. "The neighbourhood even says she never had any friends. They say she's 'self-living', and after her parents died, she was left alone."

"What about any other relatives, nephews?" asked Josh again.

"Since I've been there, I haven't heard anyone look for her."

In that time, the waiter brought the lunch, a veal steak with baked potatoes and gravy sauce. They were sitting outside as time allowed. Despite the wind, the sun was showing from time to time. Although it was still August at these latitudes, the onset of autumn was already felt. It was just over a month until Valerie was due to start her second year at university. Now she was pleased to be embarking on a practice since after just her first year of college. After they finished lunch, they both had a coffee and headed back to the city.

"I'm interested in why Mrs Mackgraver is looking for this kid now?" said Valerie, already in the car. "It has been years."

"It's obviously something to do with her youth."

"Do you know what job she had when she was young?"

"I'm not sure, but we can ask Osmond. He has lived more than 12 years in the house, and he's probably better acquainted than I am."

"All right," the inspector said, "here's the plan. After we stop by the police station to see if there's anything new, we're going to Grove Village to talk to Osmond Bolton. It would be good if we could get any new information from him."

That afternoon, Valerie was ecstatic on acting like a true investigator, and couldn't wait to tell Johnny everything. But now she wanted to know if there was any new information about Mrs Mackgraver's case. When they went through the police station, there was news from Grove Village, but it wasn't good.

Officers had searched the yard of the house and found Mrs Mackgraver's lifeless body in a thick bush of roses. They had examined it, but they found no signs of violence. There was no development in the Amalie case. Now there was a lot of work to do with the inspector, because they officially had to question everyone in the house. They had to wait until 7:00 pm when everyone came back from work and gathered in the big salon.

"Look inspector," said Osmond, he was the first one came from work. "She wasn't communicating with anyone, she wasn't a friendly woman, she was polite yes, but not friendly. Because she wanted us to pay her rent by hand, every one of us stopped by her apartment once a month to hand her the cheque, but nothing more. Sometimes she used to call Oliver Grandy to check on her, but I don't know the details. She was also seeing Marius, the gardener, but I guess so much as to pay him and explain to him what work to do. The truth is, I don't think a lot of people of people will miss her, no matter how bad it sounds. I'm more concerned about Amalie's disappearance and what will happen to us as tenants," Mr Bolton concluded.

"We have no information about Ms Druster at this time," the inspector said, "but police have been notified and we are in the process of searching. We're going to look into whether Mrs Mackgraver has written a will and eventually if she has any relatives who can inherit her property."

"She may have, but no one has ever visited her, she's been happy to live like this. From what I understand about her life, not much is known, since she almost didn't communicate with anyone, but we're going to have to investigate why someone needs to kill her if it's a murder, of course. And for now, we're going to wait for the others to come and talk to them." And then he turned to Valerie, "Let's go home because today was a tiring day."

Valerie nodded. Although it was very enticing for her to go home and dive into the bath, she had decided to make a warm cocoa and blissfully slip into her duvet.

That night, they were able to meet some of the occupants of the house. They questioned the professor, but he said nothing more than what Osmond Bolton told her. She knew nothing more than the others and had not communicated with the lady, because for all the years she lived here, she had not communicated with any of the tenants herself. The conversation with Marius was a little different.

"Tell me, Marius, when was the last time you saw Mrs Mackgraver?" the inspector asked.

"On Tuesday," the boy replied, "It was the same time when Valerie was here. I'm not involved, inspector, she was paying me good money, what am I to kill her for?"

"I didn't say you killed her," the inspector replied. "You've trapped yourself."

"Oh, no," Marius defended himself, "you said you found a body, that's why."

"Okay Marius, what were you talking about on Tuesday?" continued Karston.

"Well, the garden. That's all she and I talk about. She paid me then, and then I never saw her again."

"I'll get back to you," the inspector said.

"Well, I have nothing to stay for, I have to find a job, there's no one to pay me anymore," the gardener said.

"Until the investigation is over, you're not going anywhere," the inspector cut off.

"All right, all right, officer," a frustrated Marius said, "if I have to sit down…."

He got up to go; Valerie thought about how good the gardener looked, and how rude he was and the irony of how Osmond Bolton was an ugly but an extremely polite man.

"What do you think Valerie," the inspector asked, "is Marius guilty or at least involved in Mrs Mackgraver's death?"

"I don't think so," said the girl. "You know, inspector, one of my interesting subjects at the university is psychology. That's where they teach us how to recognise a criminal's psych profile. Frankly, Marius doesn't fall into any category at all. It's not possible, but it's unlikely. He doesn't have those qualities."

"Oh, I'm impressed with your knowledge," the inspector exclaimed, "but it's good to have suspects in mind, as there are always exceptions."

"That's right," Valerie agreed.

It was already 10:00 pm and they were both tired, and the officer offered to drive her to her apartment.

When she got home, Valerie made a warm hot chocolate and sat on the couch to drink it. Although she regretted Mrs Mackgraver's death, she thought it was a good case for her. She also wanted to understand the killer's motives and the consequences on the lives of the victims. She knew it would be hard to know all the details, but it would be interesting for her. It was midnight when she went to bed in the clean sheets and fell asleep instantly.

This morning, the inspector decided not to wake her up, and he headed to the university to interview Oliver Grandy, the chemistry assistant. He was the only one from Grove Village who wasn't questioned the night before. Oliver was working in his own lab. When he came in, the inspector found him with two students he was explaining something to.

"Hello, Inspector," said Oliver.

"Hi, Oliver, I assume you heard about Mrs Mackgraver."

"Yes, unfortunately."

"Tell me, Oliver, when was the last time you saw her. Did she talk to you?"

"Actually, the last time I saw her was a rent cheque, that was a dozen days ago."

"Haven't you seen each other since?" the inspector wondered.

"As you may know, Inspector, she wasn't very sociable. However, last year she invited me to her apartment several times. I guess she was feeling alone."

"What were you talking about when you stopped by her," the inspector asked curiously.

"Mostly questioning me about my work. She wanted me to tell her about my colleagues and my lab."

"How common were these visits?"

"Maybe twice a month, no more. But we didn't tell anyone. She insisted that we don't talk about this topic, so the lodgers don't think anything. I haven't shared with anyone either, but under the current circumstances, it's nice to know."

"Thank you, Oliver, this is some information. Let me ask you one last question? How much time did you spend at her house?"

"I can't say exactly, but sometimes about an hour, maybe. Sometimes just to have a cup of tea."

"That's it for now, Oliver. I'd ask you if you could think of anything else, please contact me."

"Sure, inspector, thanks for visiting me."

When he left, it was about 11:00 am, and Karston decided to call Valerie.

"I was at the university talking to Oliver Grandy, I'm going to tell you about it tomorrow. As you know, we have a meeting with Father Edward on Friday. I'll come pick you up at 8:00 am. Be ready."

"Okay, Inspector, I promise I'll spend all day in bed."

"Right, rest, we have a lot of work to do tomorrow. Bye for now."

"See you later," Valerie said, hanging up the phone.

It was almost noon in August, but as some English people said it was a rainy period. The weather was quite gloomy lately and it often rained. Today was no exception. The clouds had already huddled, it was only a matter of time before it rained. Valerie had everything in the fridge and really planned to spend all day in bed watching movies. It was a really good day for her. At dusk, she just got up to get her clothes ready for tomorrow, and after a while she was back in bed. She fell asleep early and the next day she was up long before 8:00 am.

She made herself a big cup of coffee, took a shower, put on thicker clothes and waited for the inspector. When he rang the doorbell, she was completely ready.

"Good morning, sir," Valery said.

The inspector looked at her from under her eyebrows.

"You know sir is not my favourite address, Valerie."

"I know, that's why I'm saying it."

"I got coffee, it's short with milk, right?"

"It's good to remember, sir," the girl smiled.

Josh started the engine and drove to the church in Durham. This morning, traffic was quite busy and their arrival time was extended. Shortly before 10:00 am, they parked the car outside the church. When they walked into the benches, there were a lot of people. At exactly 10:00 am, the morning mass began. Valerie and the inspector were forced to listen to Father Edward's 40-minute sermon. After that, he called them in. Without asking them, the father brought three cups of tea and sat at the table. He opened a notebook and handed a piece of paper to the inspector.

"As promised, Inspector. Here's the information I found in the archives."

"Tell me about this, Father? What exactly is written here?" the inspector asked.

"When Mrs Mackgraver came in at the beginning of the week, she asked about a boy christened in March, April or May 1963. According to the records, 11 children were baptised within that time. Eight of them were girls. On this sheet are the names of the three boys named here and recorded in the archive."

The inspector looked at the piece of paper:

1. Stuart Willik, born 14-03-1963 named after 31-03-1963

2. Mark Sutton, born 17-03-1963 named after 02,04,1963

3. George Peterson, born 17-02-1963, named after 7-04-1963

"It's very valuable information, Father," the officer said, "and are you aware of what happened to these children, now adult men?"

"Look," the father started, "the other day at the service, I asked the mayor about the families of these men, and he promised today at noon that he would give me their addresses if they were still in our city. But I wanted to ask you what happened to Mrs Mackgraver, did you find her?"

"I am sorry to tell you Father but my workers found her body in the thick rose bush in her garden. But there's no sign of violence on her body, and it's possible she just died of natural causes. I'm going to get a conclusion from the pathologists his afternoon, and I'll know more."

"Then I suggest you order lunch in our humble kitchen," Father Edward said, "and then when the mayor calls, you can get that information."

"Father," Valerie said, "did Mrs Mackgraver not mention why she needed the names of these guys or something to do with it?"

"Take this girl to the police, Inspector, she's not only beautiful, but she's smart," the father smiled.

"Next year she's going to be practicing for me," the inspector said.

"She didn't tell me why she was looking for them," the father turned to Valerie, "but she said she'd been looking for that information for years, but now she's looking forward to finding it."

It was approaching noon, and the inspector got a call from the police station.

"Inspector Karston, this is Peter Williams."

"Hello Peter, I'm listening."

"The autopsy results were ready, no signs of violence were found on her body, but there's something strange about it, and it's that there's an increased amount of sugars in her blood."

"What could that mean?"

"We can't say for sure, but they're likely to have diabetes and increased insulin. It would be nice to talk to her GP so we can confirm that."

"Thank you, Peter, I'll get the doctor. I've been there," the inspector said, shutting down the phone.

He passed the conversation to the father and Valerie. He didn't want to talk about the perpetrator aloud, but he thought he should continue with the investigation in this regard. Something told him it wasn't natural causes.

During this time, the father's assistant brought food, which, as the father told them, was produced in the church farm: fresh tomatoes, eggs, bacon, and bread. Father Edward also poured a small glass of red wine to excite the appetite, as he put it. They had not finished their lunch yet when the father got a pending call from the mayor. He recorded his words on a sheet, thanked him and hung up his phone. He gave the sheet of paper to the inspector exactly when everyone finished their eating.

"The food was delicious," Valerie said, "thank you, Father. I never thought you'd have a farm."

"In fact, we only produce for our own use," the father replied. "A modest amount that helps us survives, but let's goes back to the data." And he pointed at the list. The mayor said he checked all three names, first boy Stuart Willick reportedly died before he was 10. The second boy I can give you the address for, and the third, Mark Sutton, has gone to live elsewhere and his tracks are lost. According to the mayor's information, he lived on Mary Street until he was 18, and then he went to study elsewhere and never returned."

"Can I keep the sheet," the inspector asked.

"Of course, child, find out what happened to the missus. It's not right to end a human life."

"Thank you, Father, that's why we're struggling."

"And when you get the chance, stop by my abode, I'd love it."

"Bye, Father," Valerie said, and gave him a hand.

"Move on, dear girl, you'll go far."

The three of them said goodbye, and Valerie and the inspector sat in the car to discuss what was next.

"I suggest before we leave, we stop by both addresses."

The inspector started the engine and headed for Mary Street. The plan was to look for Mark Sutton's tracks, as Mrs Mackgraver had written specifically about him. They stopped in front of a large three-storey house with a large yard, away from the other houses. Mary Street was almost on the edge of town. When the inspector and Valerie called the doorbell, they didn't have to wait too long. A middle-aged woman showed up on the doorstep.

"Good afternoon," said the inspector, "we're from the police. We're investigating a case and we're interested in a man named Mark Sutton who used to live here."

"Unfortunately, my mother and father bought the house about 30 years ago. My name is Elizabeth Ardley; by the way,

I assume you're looking for the previous owners. But I don't remember much of the sale as I was about eight years old at the time."

"Could we talk to your mother or father?"

"Unfortunately, my father died, but my mother still lives here. But come in, please," she prompted them. "I'll call her now."

"Thank you, Miss Ardley."

Valerie and the inspector settled on the couch and waited for the lady to arrive. It took about 10 minutes, the door opened and a woman in her sixties entered the room. Still beautiful, her body, tall and thin. Her black hair was elegantly woven into a few white hair. She had violet eyes, a small well-formed nose, expressive lips and well-delineated eyebrows.

'She was a beauty,' Valerie thought, 'but even now in the sunset of her life, she looks beautiful.'

She was dressed in a homemade robe, white trousers with an edge and fluffy slippers. When she stepped into the room, it was like everything was on the rise.

"Good afternoon," she said, and walked toward the guests. "Would you like my daughter to make you a cup of tea?"

"No, no thank you, we just want to ask you a few questions about the previous occupants of the house."

"Yes, my daughter told me about it," Mrs Ardley said. "But I'd like you to have some tea."

Elizabeth got up and went to make some tea for her mother, and Mrs Ardley settled into a small armchair in the middle of the room.

"My family and I lived in London," Mrs Ardley began, "that's where I had my two daughters. My husband was a pharmacist at the time and he had a pretty good practice in South London. One day he received a call from a Newcastle law house, who called to tell him that his aunt had left a piece of land in Sunderland city centre. At the time, we were living on rent and it didn't stop us from moving. Michael, my husband thought it would be best to come alone and see what he could do with this land. I had two young children and it wasn't appropriate to travel with them. We wanted to see if there was a house, but it turned out that the aunt donated the house to the church."

While Mrs Ardley was talking, her daughter brought her tea. Despite the refusal, she had brought three cups for Valerie and the inspector. They thanked her and waited for the lady to continue.

"When my husband went to the law firm, they told him that a large hotel chain was interested in buying this land because it was close to the university, and also almost in the centre of the city. He called me, very excited that he would take a lot of money, and we could buy a house. Of course I was happy too; we were going to provide everything for our children. The deal was supposed to take place within a month, as there was a lot of paperwork to be done. Michael came home while he waited for the deal to end. We were young at the time, but calculating the money we would make and the expensive life we had in London, we decided it was best to move to the north. For the few days Michael was there, he said, 'he fell in love with a small town called Durham, which is close to the sea.' He told me that as we get older we will have the peace of mind of the English countryside, and our children will be able to decide where to study, as there were universities in Durham and Newcastle and Sunderland. I was determined to agree, but I wanted to see it first. When we arrived here, we rented a house nearby. I really fell in love with this city, in the small peaceful streets, in the stone buildings that seem to tell their stories. We have a castle and all kinds of beauties. You can see for yourself. When the deal was closed and we took the money, my husband bought a pharmacy on the edge of town. He started working there, but it took us about two years to find the right house to buy. The house you see belonged to a boy who had just lost his family. Me and my husband didn't see this boy because he had a solicitor. We no longer cared what happened to him. It's been about 30 years."

"I understand, Mrs Ardley," the inspector said, "and his name was Mark Sutton."

"I'm not sure, Inspector, I'm going to have to check the papers; it really was so long ago."

"If it won't be difficult for you, I'd be very grateful."

"Actually, I didn't ask you is anything wrong?"

"No, we're just looking for this guy, who is now a man, for an inheritance," the inspector lied.

He didn't want to disturb the woman because he didn't know if anyone had a hand in Mrs Mackgraver's death.

"Oh, that's great," Mrs Evelyn Ardley said. "Give me a few days, since all our papers are in the attic and my daughter will have to help me find them."

"Of course, here's my number, please call me when you're ready."

"I'll call you, Inspector."

Mrs Ardley got up to send them off. After they sat in the car, Valerie remained silent.

"What's wrong, Val?" asked Karston.

"She reminds me of someone, but I can't think of whom."

"You're right, but I guess her other child has other traits, but she was a beauty when she was young. Now, if you're not too tired, we'll go visit Mrs Mackgrave's GP."

"You know I'm not, sir," she teased. "I'm always ready for more information and investigation."

The car drove from Durham to Newcastle. During the trip, Inspector Karston called the police to ask for the name and address of the GP. It took them half an hour to get to Avenue Street to Dr Stevenson. They parked and walked into the office. Someone at the station had already called to report their visit. Dr Stevenson was 70 years old. Skipping his retirement age, he had kept practicing so he wouldn't stay home. He had greying hair, blue eyes and a slim figure. He was looking like he wasn't eating enough. His whole life had passed on Avenue Street and he wanted to stay practicing while his legs held him. He didn't have a family, and medicine was his only joy. Luckily, he was a really good doctor.

"I was expecting you. Sit down, please."

"Thank you, Dr Stevenson, thank you for taking out time," the inspector said. "I guess you know why we're here."

"Yes, yes," confirmed the doctor. "I went to the coroner because Mrs Mackgraver has been my patient for a long time, not to say for decades."

"Tell me, Doctor," asked Karston again, "do you think her death was unnatural?"

"Look, Inspector, I've had this thought through my head, too, and I'll tell you why."

"I'd appreciate it, Doctor, because this case is getting complicated."

"Mrs Mackgraver has always been a very healthy woman, but a year and a half ago, in a routine examination, I discovered that she had type 2 diabetes. She has had complaints lately, but I ignored them from the beginning and decided to run only the routine tests she was given because the sugar was not so elevated. And her condition didn't need insulin injections. I prescribed her pills. It's been a year and she came to me and said she thought the pills didn't have the desired effect and she's not feeling well. That's when I decided to change them after we did tests again, and we saw that the sugar really went up a lot. I wrote what she was allowed to eat and what she wasn't allowed to eat. About two months ago, she called me on the phone, she sounded pretty upset. She told me she was going to visit me soon because she still wasn't feeling well. I asked her if she was following everything I had prescribed, and she confirmed. Then, for the first time since I knew her, she sounded worried that she might go away, and there were still some unsettled things. I told her that she didn't have to worry, because the drugs are really good and that she has many years to live. But you saw what happened."

"Doctor," the inspector called, "what did the coroner told you?"

"That's what I wanted to tell you," the doctor replied. "I suppose you know that diabetes is incurable, but with strict adherence to recommendations and therapy, it can be controlled. The coroner and I discussed all possible options and came to the conclusion that either she did not take the pills, which is in doubt, as she was strict."

"Yes," Valerie called, "I can confirm it."

"That's right," Dr Stevenson continued, "or someone intentionally didn't give it to her."

"But how is that possible," Valerie asked, "as she lived alone? I've never seen her with anyone else in her apartment."

"But it's not a bad thing to check. It's like she never took them. And the increase in sugar can be because she has taken her banned foods more than she should have."

"I worked for her for almost a year," Valerie interrupted. "All this time, she was always so meticulous, about the way I was cleaning, to the time I was knocking on her door, to what time I would finish. I can't believe she'd be so careless about such an important thing."

"I've been treating her for years," the doctor said, "and although she never had any serious health problems," he said, "she followed all the instructions."

"Clearly," the inspector said, "so you see something suspicious, and it's our job to see if that's the case."

"You're right, Inspector, look deeper."

After the conversation was over, Valerie and Karston went to the police station. He was already almost convinced Mrs Mackgraver had been murdered, but there were more things he needed to piece together the puzzle.

Valerie came home pretty late in the evening. She wanted to call Johnny but decided not to bother him. She was going to call him for a date, straight.

As September approached and the beginning of the school year came closer, she decided to enrol in the library so she could pick up psychology books from there. The only problem was that she was running out of money and had to look for another job because Grove Village was no longer offering her anything. Valerie went to bed a little worried, but she was looking forward to tomorrow, because she would be closer to exposing the crime if there was one. Such a surprise would have given Johnny these mysteries. She could not believe that anything really happened at 148 Edmund Street.

The next day, the inspector called.

"Good morning, Val, we're going to be in Grove Village today. So when you're ready, I'll be waiting right there."

"I'll be there in an hour," Valerie replied.

"I'm waiting for you," the inspector said as he hung up the phone.

By the time she arrived at the house, Valerie saw that the officer had already entered Mrs Mackgraver's apartment.

"Good morning, miss, come on in," the officer said cheerfully, "right now, our task is to find some trace of Mrs Mackgraver's medication. Let's split the apartment in two and everyone will look in their part."

"All right, sir, let's get started."

Both took serious action with the search for the drugs or a prescription prescribed by Stevenson. After about three hours of scrubbing, they found no trace of them.

"Okay," Valerie called, since they were both already in the gym, "shouldn't there be any connection between Mrs Mackgravers death and Miss Drusterr's disappearance. It's amazing how we haven't had any connection to her for over a week."

"You're right, Val, if there's any connection between the two cases, and we should search all the apartments, right?"

"It would be nice, but where can we start first," the girl wondered.

"Let me call the D.A. I'm going to go talk to him."

When the inspector came back, he told Valerie the order would not be ready until tomorrow morning.

"Then," he continued, "our only task is to search Amalie Druster's home again. You know what we're looking for this time."

"Yes, Inspector, let's get to work."

Each began to search the apartment very carefully. They also searched the cupboards and the closet, everywhere. Neither of them found anything. It looked like Amalie had nothing to do with the old lady's death. At last, they decided to look in a cupboard in the kitchen. When Valerie opened this door, there were a lot of old pictures. Valerie leaned over to collect them, and her gaze came across a photo with four people – two adults and two children. The woman in the photo seemed extremely familiar to her. She wondered where she saw it. She showed it to the inspector to see what he thought of it.

"Look, sir, I found this in one of the cupboards," she pointed out, "doesn't the woman remind you of anyone?"

"Let me take a closer look at her," the inspector replied.

He looked closely at the photo, which was quite old. One of the children in the photo looked like the mother and the other like the father. The mother was a very beautiful woman. Even though they were clearly sisters, they didn't look alike.

"She looks familiar to me, too, but I still can't tell from where. Did you find anything else? Anything suspicious? Any tablets or prescriptions?"

"Nothing but some multivitamin box for women over 40. But that's hardly suspicious. I'm not going to let you down," the girl laughed.

"Okay, let's get this over with and go to lunch, and then we'll talk about the case."

"I'm starving anyway," Valerie rubbed her hands..

They sat in a cafeteria and ordered bacon and egg sandwiches. For Valerie, caloric food was a source of happiness, and luckily for her, whether because of her fragile growth or her metabolism, she wasn't filling up. The inspector didn't trust his metabolism and worked out hard every day at 6:00 am and 2:00 pm. By the time they had finished lunch, it had already taken four hours, Karston told Valerie that he had to go to the station because he hadn't written reports in a long time and expected to be rebuked for it.

"If you want, can I take you with me, show you the administrative work that we police do, and how it's an integral part of our job?" the inspector asked her.

"Oh, it's going to be great. I can call Johnny anyway, but he's not going to be free. Tell me what we're going to do."

"Well, the most ordinary reports. We describe where we've been and what we've done. It's not as much fun as when you're on the field. But I have to document my actions," the inspector said. "But let's go there and I'll show you every detail."

It only took 15 minutes to get to their control. Newcastle wasn't a very big city but it was very calm and beautiful. The police department was a large brick building on two floors. There was a large parking and ground floor for those temporarily arrested. When they went inside, Valerie got a little frustrated, there was almost no one in the building.

When they got to his desk, she said, "Shouldn't you have your own office, Inspector?"

"It wouldn't be bad. But I'm not that big," he replied with a smile, " I'll invite you when they give me the keys to it."

He pulled out a free chair and the two settled in.

"Let's have a cup of coffee and I'm going to show you what kind of program we're working with and how you should write your report of the day," he began to explain.

"Let me get the coffee and I'll be right there," she replied.

It was almost eight hours later when the two of them got up from the computer. All that was left in the building was the security staff.

"Don't you have job timings, inspector?" asked Valerie stretching.

"I do, but you can't just work 8 to 5 because sometimes you have to decide people's fates," he replied. "Sometimes I come home at normal times, but it happens to me rarely. That's why it's important to choose now whether this is your calling and do you really want to help people?"

"Oh, I've made up my mind, I've been dreaming it my whole life, and what you're saying won't turn me down."

"Then," he said again, and he took his jacket, "let's go so you can rest and keep your look younger for a long time."

"I think I'm getting pretty tired."

"You are now going home to rest because tomorrow we're going to the Ardleys to see how far she's come with the search for the contract."

"Wow," said Valerie happy, "we'll be back on the field. Great."

The next day at 9:00 am, Valerie was already ready, waiting for the inspector to call her and head to Durham. Before she left, she texted Johnny that they probably wouldn't see each other this week, but the latter was inviting him to his house to tell him something interesting. She hadn't told him what had happened yet because she wanted to tell him the whole story at once, and it hadn't been assembled yet. The questions were still in the air. Did someone really intentionally kill Mrs Mackgraver Where was Amalie Druster now? Who was the woman in the picture? All these issues had to be resolved and then she would tell Johnny everything and boast to him that she was involved in a real investigation. Because the thrill of practicing, she thought, has nothing to do with reading in the library. True, the books gave her knowledge, but the practice taught her on the go. As those thoughts flowed in her head, Inspector Karston called the Ardley family and Mrs Ardley confirmed the contract was in her hands.

"I'm waiting for you, Inspector, with your charming assistant," Mrs Ardley said kindly.

"Thank you, ma'am, we'll be there in an hour."

By the time the inspector went to Valerie's block, she was already completely ready. They went through the usual place to grab coffee and headed straight to Mary Street, the street where the lady lived. On the door they were welcomed again by Elizabeth, and after greetings were exchanged she introduced them to her mother, who had positioned herself on the sofa in the drawing room and waited for them with a folder of documents.

"It's good to see you again," Ms Ardley began, finding the document and the deed of the house. "Like I told you, I keep a lot of papers in the attic, and it would be hard for me to check everything myself. Make yourself comfortable, please," she points out the places, "and Elizabeth will prepare us tea and bring it to us."

"But, please," the inspector said, "we're not going to hold on much, we just want to see the documents."

"No matter what," the lady objected, "let's give you something."

When Elizabeth served the tea, Mrs Ardley, who had previously told more stories about moving them to Newcastle, opened the file and was surprised.

"I haven't reviewed these documents in a long time," she said.

She pulled every single document out of the folder and began to unravel them.

"You know," she continued, "it's a little weird, but it turns out I don't know where their originals are. I hope these will work for you, too. She picked the deed and handed it to the inspector."

"Don't worry, Mrs Ardley," the inspector said, "we only care about the seller's name. After I turned on the signature page, it really turned out that the seller was Mark Sutton. The question was why Mrs Mackgraver had mentioned that name to Father Edward."

The inspector carefully reviewed the document and returned it to the missus.

"Where do you think the original went?" the officer asked.

"I have no idea," Evelyn replied, "the last time I saw him was 18 years ago, when my husband died. We needed to transfer the inheritance of the house."

"What happened to the pharmacy you mentioned?" the inspector asked again.

"Oh, it's a long story, but in general, 10 years before my husband left, we lost almost everything. So from the lavish life we led, all of a sudden we had to try to make ends meet."

"I'm sorry to hear that."

Mrs Ardley sounded upset, she tried to suppress the tears in her eyes, but it was very difficult for her. She reopened the folder and started pulling pictures.

"Look at that inspector," she tweeted. "This photo is from the time we had everything. And now even my home isn't entirely ours, because it's mortgaged."

The photo was of two young people who looked very happy. When Valerie looked at the photo, it suddenly flashed to her, so it was the woman in Amalie Druster's photo. She didn't say anything. There was about half an hour left, during which time Mrs Ardley spoke with sadness about their lives during a time when everyone lived well. Valerie couldn't wait to be alone in the car to tell him about this discovery, as it would surely have tilted the investigation in a new direction, and they could have revealed the truth. For Valerie, revealing the truth would have been the best ending of the summer.

"Inspector," Valerie started enthusiastically when they were both in the car. Outside weather had become quite chilly and Valerie was shaking.

"What happened with you when you saw, Mrs Ardley's photo?"

"It wasn't really her photo, it was the image she showed us," the girl replied. "Did you notice the people in her picture?"

"Yes," the inspector said indefinitely.

"Did you see anything?"

"No, nothing but some people."

"Inspector, the woman in the photo is the same as the woman in Miss Amalie Druster's photo."

"Are you sure? This will definitely lead us to a new line of investigation."

"I'm sure, but you have to take the picture and compare it," Valerie replied. "When you saw the portrait in the apartment, didn't the woman remind you of anyone?"

"Yes, you may be right, dear girl," the inspector is pleased, "apparently Amalie looks like her mother, who is still very beautiful."

"I guess Elizabeth looks like her father."

"Probably. I suggest we move as fast as we can to get the picture and go back and interview Mrs Ardley about her daughter."

"It's going to be exciting," Valerie said.

As they returned to Grove Village, the sky went dark and it started raining like hell. The time until they got to the house seemed endless to them because of the traffic and the rain. Valerie walked into apartment No 5 and took the photo just before she walked into the kitchen as if she heard some noise. She started looking around.

"Is anyone here?" she stared. But she didn't get any response. She decided to check the rooms, but she couldn't find anyone. So she went, took the picture and went out.

"You know, Inspector, I was surprised when I walked into the apartment," Valerie began as she got into the car. "I thought I heard some noise inside."

"Are you sure?" the inspector asked.

"No, that's why I'm saying it seemed like that to me."

"So let's not pay attention, let's go to Mrs Ardley again, I'm interested in whether she's aware that her daughter is missing?" asked Josh Karston.

"Are you going to ask her?"

"Yes," the inspector replied, and he started the car's engine. "I'm going to have to stay up late at the police station tonight," he complained, "Do you want to come help me?"

"I don't have much to do, and I don't want to go home that early."

"I can dictate the report and you write it."

"I'll help you any way I can."

The two went to the house in Durham. When they knocked on the door and Mrs Ardley showed up, she was pretty surprised to see them again.

"I wasn't expecting you again, and my daughter went to work, so I'm opening up," she said.

"As you know, we're doing an investigation, and our current arrival is related to that."

"But please come in," Mrs Ardley interrupted, "let's not stand at the door. I'll make tea and we can talk in peace."

Valerie and the inspector went in and settled straight on the couch. Within minutes, the lady brought the tea and sat across from them.

"I will listen to you carefully," she began.

"Today, shortly after we left your house, my assistant Valerie drew attention to a fact. You have shown a picture of you from the years when you were financially satisfied and happy. And we found almost the same picture in the apartment of a woman, which is located in the house where we are investigating."

Valerie took the picture out and handed it to Mrs Ardley. When she was picked up, the elderly woman looked at her and tears flowed down her sides.

"That's you, Mrs Ardley," Inspector Karston asked.

"It's me with my family, my two daughters and my husband when we were really happy."

"What's your other daughter's name, Mrs Ardley?" the inspector asked again.

"Her name is Amalie. We named her by that name because my husband said it sounded beautiful."

"That's right," the officer said, "and do you know she lives in Grove Village in Newcastle, with Mrs Mackgraver?"

"I had no idea, Inspector. Amalie and I haven't spoken in over three years. The last time she came home asking for money from me and Elizabeth, I replied that with Betty's salary, we could barely pay the mortgage, and my pension was used to feed us. Then she told me I had ruined her life, slammed the door and never saw her again."

"And in the meantime, have you heard anything about her? Did anyone in town talk or call your town to speak with her or did she call you?

"You know, Inspector, I go to church service every Tuesday at 10:00. It's been my habit for years. That morning I was talking about, Amalie came to see her sister and told her she was looking for some documents."

"When was that?"

"Somewhere about a year ago, Betty told me she looked pretty good. She came because she forgot the papers, that's what she said, nothing more."

"I understand," the inspector said, "thank you very much for the information."

"You don't think anything happened to her," Ms Ardley said.

"No, ma'am, when we searched her apartment, nothing seems to be like this, don't worry."

"Thank you, Inspector, I'd appreciate it if you'd let me know when you find her. Despite everything we've been through, she's my firstborn daughter."

"I just want to ask you one last question, ma'am. Amalie Druster, is she married because, as far as I know, she was alone in the house."

"She was married, Inspector, to Stuart Druster, they got married when she was just 18 years old. He was rich, and she was always looking for a rich man. He was 35 years old at the time, they lived in a big house, they had servants. After about 5 years, down multiple attempts it turned out that my daughter could not have children. Stuart was very disappointed and left her. He didn't leave her any money, just a small house in the country, but she sold it to get money. Unfortunately, Inspector, even though she's my daughter, Amalie is my nightmare for me. A wonderful little creature was born, but she became an extremely selfish and cruel woman." Mrs Ardley sobbed.

"Unfortunately," the officer said, "our good intentions don't always turn into action. I hope we didn't upset you very much, Mrs Ardley."

"Don't worry, Inspector, everyone pays for their own mistakes. But like I said, she's my daughter, and I'm asking you to just tell me what happened, when you find out?"

Valerie and Josh got up to leave, and Mrs Ardley went to send them off. As they shook hands, Valerie shook the lady's hand in a show of support. They got in the car and drove to Newcastle Police Station. Along the way, the whole conversation was about the lady.

"Inspector, do you think Amalie Druster was somehow involved in Mrs Mackgraver's death?" asked Val.

"Honestly, I don't know, after hearing these words from her own mother, I'm starting to think there's something," the inspector replied.

He stared at the trees along the highway. The rain had already stopped and it was as if he had washed everything. The greenery looked so fresh, and the sky was clean and calm. As always in life, he thought, something good eventually happens.

"But she's such a beautiful woman," Valerie said, "it would be a shame to be involved."

"It would be Val, but very often appearances can lie, and it turns out that on the inside, beautiful people are often not very good, unfortunately. But let's get to the station. There we will be able to solve the puzzle and we can come up with a solution. Don't forget, tomorrow we'll have a warrant to search the rest of the apartments."

"Oh, I'm looking forward to it," Valerie replied. "Inspector," she added, "we didn't eat anything today."

"You're right," he replied, "we have a chair in the office and they cook well there, we'll pick up something and sit down to work."

Valerie nodded her head and sank into her own thoughts. It rained in the afternoon when they ordered the last two steaks with potatoes from the police chair. When they finished eating, they went up to his desk and sorted out the reports from the past days. Inspector Karston left Valerie alone so he could talk to his boss about the case. It took more than an hour for his boss to hear all the details of the investigation. Meanwhile, Valerie had read and arranged all the reports of the last three weeks. When the inspector showed up at the desk, she greeted him with a broad smile.

"Did you find anything new, Val?" he asked her.

"I haven't really found it, but I thought of something that might be of great importance," the girl replied.

"I'm listening to you very carefully," the inspector replied with a smile.

"I have a friend I share everything with. A few weeks ago, we sat and drank coffee. I told him about the occupants of the house and told him that the professor works at the university, and he said that in the evening he would go to a university professors' party and work as a waiter. After we met the next week, he told me that many of his colleagues had talked about a guest who was a scary piece, as he put it. I asked him who she was with, but he couldn't answer me. In this case, I am sure that it was Miss Amalie, but I do not know who she was with, since I later found out that Oliver Grandy, the principal assistant, also works at the university in the department of chemistry."

"Val, this is very good news. I'm not going to say that," the inspector said, "which gives us a reason to question the professor and the assistant today, without waiting for the search warrant tomorrow."

"Really?" asked Valerie, "can we do it now."

"Not only can we do that, but we better get going. It's six o'clock, I guess everyone will be home from work soon," the inspector replied.

At 6:40 pm, they'd already arrived at the house. It was still bright out there. Only traffic in the city had slowed them down. They decided to question the assistant first, as he was about the same age as Miss Druster. They had to wait for him because he hadn't come home from university yet. When they walked into the salon, they found Osmond Bolton.

"Hello, Mr Bolton," said Valerie, greeting him.

"Hi, Valerie, Inspector," he said.

"Did you learn anything about the building?" the inspector asked.

"From what I understand, we have a month before the property is handed over to the municipality, because from what I understand Mrs Mackgraver, there are no heirs," Osmond said, "You've heard anything else?"

"No Mr Bolton, we're still doing an investigation," Karston replied, "and Valerie helps me a lot."

"Oh, I'm sure, she's a great girl."

"Mr Osmond," Valerie called, flattered by the compliment. "Do you remember when Miss Amalie had to go to the university party?"

"Sure, Valerie, why do you ask?" Osmond wondered.

"I want to ask, who invited Amalie to the party?"

"As far as I can remember, the professor, but why are you interested," Bolton asked Valerie and the inspector looked at each other.

"In truth, Mr Bolton, it's probably somehow related to Mrs Mackgraver's death."

"I'm not going to lie to you," Osmond replied, "As far as I know, she died of natural causes."

"Maybe, somewhat, but not exactly," Valerie said.

"You're confusing me, you two," Osmond smiled kindly.

"Look, Mr Bolton, I can't tell you everything, but I guess soon we'll all know what happened, and I hope we find Miss Amalie Druster."

"I'm glad you told me what you could," Osmond replied. "If I have to wait, I will wait."

"Do you know when the professor usually comes home?" the inspector asked again.

"It's normal," Osmond said, "but of course he's sometimes late."

"I'd like to talk to him," the inspector said.

Just when the inspector said that, the professor flew into the salon, wet and nervous.

"Remember what I told you, Osmond," he began without even noticing the guests. "I didn't even know he could play me like that."

The professor sat on the couch. The inspector approached him, and it was as if the professor was suddenly getting away with it.

"Oh, Inspector, I didn't even notice you, excuse me."

"I'd like to talk to you alone."

"No problem," the professor replied, "what's this all about?"

"I'm going to leave you alone," Osmond interjected, "if you need anything, I'm in my apartment," Osmond Bolton came out of the gym, and the only people left inside was the professor, Valerie and the policeman.

"I'm listening, Inspector," the professor began, "is it important?"

"Actually," Karston replied, "As far as we found out a few weeks ago, there was a party at the university where you work. You went with Miss Amalie Druster, is that true?"

"Why do you care about that?" the teacher wondered.

"I'm going to ask you to answer that question."

"Look, we had a party at the university some time ago for the student graduation professors. The truth is, I've wanted to invite Miss Druster for a while, since she seemed to be giving me some signals, so I invited her to that ball. She came and was irresistible, but she didn't stay with me for long," the professor said, and it was as if his whole being was disappointed, "Inspector, I'm a naïve old fool," he added sadly. "But anyway, to answer your question directly, I did go with Amalie Druster."

"Did you talk about anything special with the lady," the inspector asked again.

"I tried to talk to her about literature, but she interrupted me all the time and made it clear to me that she wanted me to introduce her to Oliver."

"Who's Oliver?" the inspector asked again.

"Oliver Grandy, the assistant."

"What's she going for?"

"I have no idea, Inspector, when we got there, Oliver showed up about an hour later, and I introduced her, she turned around, grabbed him by hand, and I never saw her again."

"I understand, Professor, let me ask you one last question. Have you known Oliver Grandy for a long time?"

"I can say so," Mr Brighton replied, "we've been working in one place for a long time, but we've never really communicated. I don't like him as a person, and the difference in years is obvious."

"Thank you, can we contact you again if we need you?"

"As you can see, I didn't escape. If there's anything, just call me in the gym."

Valerie and the inspector left the professor's apartment.

"I really felt sorry for him," Valerie said.

"Yes, but still Amalie is not a spoon for his mouth," the officer replied.

"But then why did she agree to go out with him?" the girl again asked.

"It was probably a step to get to the assistant. Women are insidious, Valerie, especially when they want to achieve something important for them."

"That sounds sexist, inspector, but maybe it's true," she laughed.

"Oh, trust me, I have more experience."

When they walked into the gym again, Osmond was still there.

"Are you done with the investigation," he asked them.

"We have another point, but maybe we will do it tomorrow."

"I hope it all ends well," Osmond smiled.

"I have hope too Mr Bolton, but I doubt it," the inspector said.

Detective Inspector Josh Karston had doubts and decided the best option was to wait until tomorrow for the assistant's interrogation. He grabbed Valerie by the hand and they left the house.

"Look, Valerie, we're tired today, let's go home, and tomorrow morning we'll come back and move on."

"But isn't this the time now?" resisted Valerie, "so we can catch him in the middle."

"No, Val, we'll wait till tomorrow. I have something in mind," the inspector insisted.

"Whatever you say, boss," Valerie agreed, "but I think we're in the final stage."

"I hope so," the officer replied. "Now I'm going to drive you home, and tomorrow I'll be waiting for you here at 7:00 am, so we can catch him before he goes to work."

"I'll be here at 7:00 am," the girl replied.

When they met again at 7:00 am in the salon of the house, the warrant from the prosecutor for the search of the two apartments was not yet ready. But the inspector was pleased to knock on Oliver Grandy's door. After the tenth tap, Oliver appeared at the door, sleepy and angry.

"What happened here, gentlemen?" he asked officially.

"I need to ask you a few questions, Mr Grandy. You remember me; I hope, Inspector Karston of Newcastle Police, and Valerie Smith, my assistant."

Valerie was flattered that the officer called her his assistant.

"All right, come on in," Oliver said.

He was a small, unfazed man, and without glasses, he looked like a diver.

"I'm going to go make some coffee and listen to you, Inspector," Grandy said.

"Okay, but hurry up, I don't have much time," the inspector replied.

After a dozen minutes, when the coffee was ready, Oliver was dressed and washed, he sat at the table quite calmly to talk to the inspector.

"What's this about, Inspector Karston?"

"When we spoke last time, you didn't tell me you knew Miss Druster more closely."

"I know her from here because she's my neighbour," Oliver lied.

"And we have information that you had a closer relationship. Look, Mr Grandy, it would be good to tell us the truth, or we can charge you with her disappearance."

At that moment, the inspector's phone rang. His conversation took exactly three minutes. He got up and called Valerie out in the hallway.

"Listen, Val," he started, "things are getting really interesting."

"What happened, Inspector?" asked the girl with curiosity.

"I just got a call from the office, and I got word that the notary had a request filed this morning that Miss Amalie Druster had a will in her name for Grove Village."

"What?" stared Valerie. "You mean she inherits the house?"

"Yes, a document signed personally by Mrs Mackgraver."

"But how is that possible," Valerie asked. "She's been living here for a year."

"It just got really tangled up."

"What are you going to do?"

"Let's finish the interrogation with Oliver, hear what else he has to say, and then we'll see what we do."

"Let's go in then," he pulled Valerie by the elbow.

Oliver Grandy hadn't moved off the table. When they came in, he looked at them with anticipation.

"All right, Oliver, let's get back to our conversation. Tell me, you know Amalie very well."

"Not as good as I'd like," he replied grimly.

Then he told about the party, how everyone was competing to invite Miss Druster to dance, how she had honoured everyone with attention, how she misled him and the professor that she was interested, and how he regretted trusting her.

"And you know that Miss Druster has a will that she's the heir to Grove Village."

"I had no idea," Oliver said, getting up from the chair and nervously walking around the kitchen. "But how could she? She could not stand Mrs Mackgraver."

"Do you know where Miss Druster might be right now?"

"I may have some idea, but I'm not sure."

******

The month of September was extremely favourable to the island, the sun was shining high, the temperatures were normal and the humidity was not so high. It was less than a week until the start of the second year in the Valerie Smith department. It had been less than a month of action in Grove Village. Because she didn't have that good of a memory, she was writing down all the time in her diary about what was going on with the investigation. Last Tuesday, Johnny called her, and she invited him to her guest suite. They ordered a meal, and she pulled out the diary.

"Tell, Val, it must have been very exciting," he began.

"Too bad you weren't here, I can't tell you everything," she frowned.

"I know, I know, but for this holiday, I've been raising money all summer," he said. "Now, how did it all end and why did you tell me you were profitable?"

Valerie opened the diary and started reading.

August 1, 2017

I was anxious to find out about Miss Druster. That's when I decided to contact the missus and learn how she lived over the years. The truth is, I wanted to put together as much the puzzle as possible. Why had Mrs Mackgraver gone like that? Why is Miss Amalie Druster missing? What about the house and its occupants? I had to answer those questions, which is why I went to talk to the lady so I could start somewhere? She had retired already, and she really didn't mind if we talked, I told her that the inspector sent me, which was kind of a white lie. But she didn't say no, on the contrary she was happy. And so I convey her story in my own words. I hope credible enough:

As I have already told you, me, my husband and two daughters, Amalie and Elizabeth, moved to this part of England for the sake of inheritance. He, at that time in the 1980s, had made one of the most successful pharmacies in this area, we also bought this house with five bedrooms and a huge yard. Our children grew up satisfied with everything. The only reason I wanted to work was social life. Durham is not a very big city, and I was a young woman and needed social communication. Since I had graduated from college with an accounting profile, I was offered a part-time job at the University of Sunderland. I was happy; I had a job and friends. My kids got the best of everything, but they were very different. When we moved, Amalie was six years old, Betty was three. Amalie was confident, while Elizabeth was quite shrouded and insecure. Amalie was growing up a very beautiful child and I think she understood it, she used every occasion to make a profit from it. Betty, on the other hand, didn't have her sister's beauty, and she felt depressed. Our whole life was very happy and everything was in a right place I never even dreamed of such luxury. My big and beautiful house once a month was gathering the elite of the North, if the weather was nice, we would have a garden party, if not our drawing room was big enough to bring the selected guests together. We just had a wonderful life. My husband used to hire cleaners so his girls wouldn't strain, as he said. That's how the years went. When they weren't at school, by the way, my children were studying at a private school, so when they didn't attend classes, they liked to go to their father's pharmacy, which was an extremely large room. In the 1980s, many of the drugs were made in the pharmacy itself by trained pharmacists. The kids would sit there and watch their preparation. Amalie would come back at night and say that when she grew up, she would be in the same field. My husband and I had a very nice relationship, I was an attractive woman, and he was a very friendly man. One day, when we were all gathered around the dinner table and my husband had already hired a cook to make us delicious meals. He told me that Mr Mackgraver was one of our acquaintances in Newcastle, a lawyer by profession...

"Wait, wait," he interrupted, "is she talking about Mrs McGraw's father?"

"Listen without interrupting me, Joe, and you'll find out," Valerie, answered him quickly.

...... As I said, a lawyer by profession. He told him that he could put money into an enterprise and buy shares. I don't know if you've heard this maxim that the human eye is insatiable. We discussed it, and we both thought it would be an adventure to put our money in stocks. At the time, we were both in our mid-30s and we loved adventures. We were very happy to be offered something new. For a few years in a row,

Mr Mackgraver was advising us on where it would be best to invest. We did it and won, and with the money we went around almost the whole world. To have time for trips and restaurants, I quit my job and indulged in vanity. It was 1985, when Amalie was in school. Shortly before the school year began, my husband invested a large amount of money in a London firm. It's been a few months, and a few days before Christmas, we found out that the company had gone bankrupt. And we were left with nothing but duties. Although we were never close to Mr Mackgraver, my husband went to tell him about the situation. But the lawyer only lifted his shoulders and said that the business world has always been cruel and that he never guaranteed that we will always be on top. The duties had begun to put pressure on us. We were forced to mortgage the pharmacy and the house. Drug makers showed up everywhere. I tried to get back to work, but because I hadn't practiced for years, I was turned down. And I couldn't do anything else. I had lived for years just to show myself. My daughters were excluded from the private school because we couldn't pay the fees. Amalie was furious. Elizabeth took it normally. My eldest daughter was so disappointed in us that one night she turned around and told me she hated me. It hurt, but then I didn't realise that in the years I didn't demand anything from them, but I gave them everything. I didn't talk to them; I was paying for a psychologist. I paid for everything related to my children.

They grew up and we became estranged. Amalie was 18 at the time, with only a few months left to finish. She was about to go to university. She was a beauty with black thick hair, great eyes and a slender body. The problem was she had no feelings for anyone. The only thing that mattered to her was to have money and to live the way she lived until now without anyone messing with her. After you told me she hated me, she packed her bags and ran away. She wrote us a letter not to look for her, since she won't come back until we get rich. She later told me that she had married a rich man, but because she didn't have a child, he divorced her. From that marriage, she had inherited a small house and kept his last name. Over the years, she would come, but quickly walked away, frustrated that we were no longer wealthy. My young daughter Elizabeth and I are paying off the mortgage. A few years ago, my husband got sick and died. It's just me and Elizabeth now. You know, Valerie, I've been thinking a lot about where we went wrong and why we got here? I came to the conclusion that their father and I left them to fate, did not talk to them, did not include in our lives, they had no duties but to look good. And they looked good, but nothing more. It was the fact that Amalie was more emotional and intimate, her fall was greater. I know it's my fault because I'm her mother, but there's nothing you can do anymore. Some time ago, she came again to ask us for money because she found some kind of gold mine and would soon have the same fame and the same money as before. Then she picked up a big scandal and left. I haven't seen or heard from her since.

"I recorded this as a story from Mrs Ardley, Joe, and it turns out the two families knew each other."

"Very exciting, three hands, and what happened next?"

"Wait, I'll tell you about it. Don't spoil the surprise," he got grilled by Valerie.

94

August 15th, 2017

After our conversation with Oliver Grandy, the chemistry assistant, which was supposed to be about 30 minutes long, and it took a few hours, we were able to find out where Amalie Druster was. A significant reason for our success was that Miss Druster had missed an important clue, and it was that she was trying to charm all the men, but she was giving them nothing. She's been hanging out with Oliver Grandy for a few months now, and he wanted revenge. I'm going to save some details and methods for the inspector so I don't embarrass him, and I'm going to reveal the location of Miss Druster in the last few weeks. According to precise instructions from Mr Grandy, we found her in the lofts of Grove Village. At first, he was in a good spirits. Her long thick black hair was lifted high in a ponytail, her pretty face was without a drop of make-up, her attire was simple homemade, but well enough accentuated her slender figure. I think the inspector was also captivated by it, but he quickly shook his head back and started with the questions. At the beginning of the conversation, she denied that she knew Mrs McGraw and that she knew anything, although it was quite difficult for her to explain why she wasn't in her apartment, but in the attic. She claimed the reason was that she felt safer here, and she didn't want anyone to know that she was isolated. She gave ridiculous explanations to the inspector's questions. However, he began to lose patience and pressed her into the corner, figuratively speaking, and then she succumbed. And now I'm going to try very precisely to recreate her story:

'As you know my name is Amalie Druster on Father Ardley, my life started as a fairy tale, I was born in London, but when I was five my parents moved to Durham. My dad *opened a pharmacy, we bought a huge house with a yard, and I had all the toys in the world. I got enrolled in a private school. All my classmates had money, I had friends, but only from school, because the other were very ordinary. I have a sister who is much different from me, even though she had every reason to be as special as me. Over the years, my father would take me from time to time at the pharmacy, and I quickly soaked up how drugs are made and what medicine it is for. I grew up a beautiful girl like my mother and was used to being paid attention. The truth is that our parents didn't have much time for us, as they were busy throwing parties or collecting luggage for another trip around the world. And if someone complained, my mother and father could always pay to keep quiet. My sister was much different, shrug and ordinary like I said, so we weren't very close, and she wasn't very pretty. By the time I was 15, I was already spinning the boys on my finger, not splitting their bass at all, going out with them, but demanding respect for what I was entitled to. That's how my days went in carefree and joyful. Until one day I found out my father had lost a huge amount of money. Things went down very sharply. My parents started making savings, and I didn't like that at all. That same year, I was about to graduate and go to study in London. I had my own plans, and all of a sudden everything collapsed. Mr Mackgraver was dad's adviser on where to put his money. Shortly before I graduated, I was kicked out of private school for unpaid contributions, I was furious at everyone, at my father, at Mr Mackgraver, at my sister. The anger at my sister came because she took things very calmly. My mother offered to move me to a normal school, but I, Amalie Ardley, a beauty and a rich woman to go to the mere mortals, absurd. It didn't* take long for me to meet my future husband, Mr Druster, a charming, wealthy man, 15 years older than me. We were married for four years, and I couldn't have a child with him. I had everything to make me feel really good. I didn't finish my education and I didn't work. I had a maid, we had parties and I was brilliant. One day my husband told me he wanted to get a divorce. Just like that. I was shocked. I didn't want to be out of money again. Then I wanted to agree with him on alimony, and I also wanted the big house we lived in. But he categorically refused, and I hated him for life. The only thing he left me was a small two-bedroom house.'

This is where Ms Druster cried bitterly. Although she was a very confident woman–she was clearly in a spirited way, too.

I still sympathised with her, but after hearing a remnant of the story, I definitely stopped liking her. But listen to what happened next.

'After my divorce, I was only 21, I decided to return home. My sister had started working as a kindergarten assistant. And my mom was looking for a job. Our father had already grown ill, so they were forced to mortgage our big house because the costs went up enormously. I couldn't work, of course. I wasn't born for this. For me, the job was a humiliation. I had to come up with something to get rich from. It had been a while. At some point, though, I already knew what I wanted to do. I hadn't thought of it before. It occurred to me to contact Mr Mackgraver and ask for the money my late father lost because of him. I decided to go straight to visit him and ask for my money. I knew where he lived, and I *remembered him, too. One day I got on the bus and went that way. I didn't tell anyone. I had some money because the house my husband left me was rented out. When I arrived in the city, I found out from neighbours that Mr Mackgraver had died, but his wife and daughter lived there. I rang the doorbell and Mrs Mackgraver opened the door for me. I was internally disappointed that I couldn't get my money directly, but I was determined that I would achieve what I could. Turns out they both had no idea about Mr Mackgraver's business. But for them, he had left a great legacy. Mr Mackgraver's daughter was 45 years old and was not married, even though she had a lot of money. To tell you the truth, she was neither beautiful nor had any other qualities. Besides, her mother wanted her to be able to run the house on Edmund Street. We got close. From time to time, they organised gatherings because I was bored anyway. Very often I stayed there and had learned the location of the house well. I knew how to get to every room and apartment, to the attics too. Young Mrs Mackgraver was very meticulous. I guess because of the life she'd led, closed and boring, she'd built up some weird habits. There was always a place in them, and when she and her mother went out, they wore gloves, dressed in the most ridiculous way. They were a strange couple, bored to brain on their bones, but they had money.*

She was already quite old. It didn't take long and she's was gone. For Mrs Mackgraver, that seemed to be the end. She had lived close to her mother all her life. She was lost. She stopped the gatherings, she hung up, there were almost no lodgers anymore. One day she told me she wanted to talk. We sat in her perfectly arranged apartment. After her mother's death, she had become even more meticulous. She started telling me a story:

She was an only child, raised by conservative parents who wanted her obedience and order, had lived like this all her life. She was prepared for her husband, but she never found the right one for her. At 17, she was sent to study at Durham Accounting. That's how she was going to help distribute the money in Grove Village. A girl, untouched by a male hand, she began to get carried away by her professor of statistics. She was never pretty, but she was very young at this time. The 55-year-old professor, was not only her teacher but also became her mentor. One day, in a moment of weakness, he seduced her. That's when she gets pregnant, but she can't tell anyone. Very soon after, the professor had a heart attack and died. Mrs Mackgraver got into trouble. She could not bring such shame to her highly respected family by giving birth to an illegitimate child. So after learning of her pregnancy, Mrs Mackgraver interrupted her studies and went to Chester Le Street. There, she gave birth to a son named Mark Sutton and left him in the hospital. That's where his tracks get lost. She can't look for him while her parents are alive, as that would be a big blow to them. From her guilt, she becomes even more meticulous. After her mother died, she went to look for the traces of her forgotten child. And she found them. She finds the birth certificate and tracks where he was baptised. She's got a lot of money, and a lot of people get chatty after a few quid given to them. So after a long time looking for her son, who turned out to be 50 years old at the time, she discovered that he had lived in our family home in Durham. The family that adopted him is the same one that my parents bought the

house from. And so the wheel spins. I grew up. If she found
this man, he would become the only heir.

"This is where I interrupted her story, Joe, and I tell you what the inspector and I actually found. I don't know if she figured it out, but in fact, her long-lost child turned out to be Osmond Bolton, who was adopted by a very good family at the time. They were at the age of adopting him after losing their son in a car accident. When he turned 18 they both died within a few months. Then he decided to sell the big house where Amalie lived because he was very lonely there. Over the years, he could not find a partner to supplement him and remained single. He works as a statistician, like his biological father. Mrs Mackgraver understands that Osmond Bolton is her son and very much wants all the property to remain for him, at least in a sense to be able to make up for her absence. Amalie also knows that Mrs Mackgraver is already suffering from diabetes and has a treacherous thought of getting rid of the lady quickly and taking all the properties as she is entitled to. With the help of assistant Grandy, she took a placebo pill and replaced her insulin on pills with the placebo pill. That way, Mrs Mackgraver feels pretty bad every day to the point where she falls into the garden. She didn't directly kill her. Because Amalie knows where the lady's docs are, she takes the will and records it in her name. No one knows that Mrs Mackgraver had a son. When we went to Amalie this morning, she was convinced she'd get the will. But that's not how it happened. I most solemnly told Osmond he was a rich heir. He wasn't that excited because he thought Mrs Mackgraver was not a good woman. But what you promised me was to leave me at work if I wanted to live in the house and not pay rent. As it turned out, the fact that he's not the most beautiful man on earth has nothing to do with his moral hoods."

"So, Johnny, I'm going to live and work on Edmund Street, and I'm going to have to do it."

"That's a great story, Valerie." Johnny said, and he poured more coffee on both of them.

End of part one.